A Recomme
by tl
Iditarod Educati

D1550051

Dogsled Dreams

"Any teacher using Gary Paulsen's *Woodsong* would want Terry Johnson's *Dogsled Dreams*. Terry's realistic writing style and word choice bring the reader through experiences that bring emotions to the surface ... emotions of real life living with sled dogs."

– Diane Johnson, Iditarod's Education Director

"A warm, coming-of-age story about hopes and dreams, but most of all, finding the true meaning of family and friends, whether they have two legs or four!"

– Darcy Johns, Youth Services Librarian,
Cole Harbour, Nova Scotia

"...demonstrates the bond between mushers and their dogs, the devotion mushers feel for their dogs, and the lengths to which they will go to ensure their dog's health and well-being."

– Pam Flowers, *Alone Across the Arctic: One Woman's Epic Journey by Dog Team*

"Exhilarating … It's very easy to get lost in the pages."
— Lisa Barker, BiblioReads.com

"Rebecca and her dogs not only came alive, but they brought me along on their adventures."
— Cynthia Chapman Willis, author of *Dog Gone and Buck Fever*

"As a father to a young girl, I was thrilled to see Rebecca have such high hopes and dreams for herself and to see her father support her … This is a beautiful story both dads and their daughters can enjoy reading and discussing together!"
— Chris Singer, Book Dads.com

"Johnson's intimate knowledge of the dogs she describes is real, heart-warming, and often humorous … This is a high-impact story that both elementary and secondary teachers can use in their classrooms to engage at-risk readers."
— Teri Treftlin, Secondary School Teacher, Geraldton, Ontario

follow your dreams

Dogsled Dreams

Terry Lynn Johnson

Edmond, Oklahoma

Dedication

For Denis, Rebecca, and Victoria.
Everything good in my characters is inspired by you.

4RV Publishing LLC.; PO Box 6482; Edmond, OK 73083
http://4rvpublishingllc.com

Illustrations Copyright © 2010 Aidana WillowRaven and 4RV Publishing
Book design by Aidana WillowRaven

ISBN-13: 978-0-9826423-4-4

Printed in Canada

Part One

Puppies

Chapter One

Rebecca whipped past snow-covered spruce, their dark trunks only a few feet from her on either side. The sled hit a ridge on the trail and flew, airborne for a giddy moment before it crunched back down.

Who needs roller coasters when you've got sled dogs, thought Rebecca. She grinned and felt her face crinkle in the cold air.

She wore her anorak, deerskin mitts, and ski goggles. The goggles fogged up, so she held her breath. She didn't want to miss anything.

"You warm enough, Becca?" her dad asked. He stood behind her on the runners as he mushed the team.

"Yeah, Dad. You just pay attention to what you're doing." Rebecca eyed the nearby trees.

They approached a tight bend in the trail and

she glanced behind at the rooster tail of snow that fanned out.

"Apollo, gee!" her dad called.

Apollo reached the fork in the trail and veered right without hesitation. This way led them straight home. Rebecca wished her dad had said 'haw', instead. Then they'd take the longer trail.

She wiped her nose with the back of her mitt, and studied the gait of the lead dogs. Apollo and Blaze trotted together shoulder to shoulder, two perfectly matched Alaskan Huskies. Apollo's white feet flashed at the ends of long black legs. From her position in the sled, Rebecca knew that his fierce blue eyes fixated on the trail ahead. Apollo's intensity while he ran made Rebecca smile. She didn't care if all her friends from school made fun of his homely face. To her, Apollo was wonderful. All the dogs were.

"Weren't we supposed to be going for a long run today, Dad?"

"You've got to get back to the homework you promised you'd do yesterday."

Oh yeah. "But I've got lots of time. It's only a little math." *Only about a thousand pages of math. Grade seven math sucks, big time.*

They broke from the trees and onto the creek that they crossed every training run.

"And after you finish your math, you said you'd help me with— BLAZE! On by! Apollo, NO!"

"Dad! Look out!"

A fat beaver sat on the ice right on the trail. His shiny head jerked up as the team pounded closer.

Rebecca's dad hollered. He threw down the snow hook, but too late.

The dogs reached the beaver.

Rebecca watched with mouth agape as the large rodent lunged at Apollo. He sank his long, yellow teeth into the dog's leg. Apollo shrieked. The sound made the bottom of Rebecca's stomach drop. She jumped out of the sled. Apollo snapped at his opponent, but he missed as the sleek animal disappeared under a hump in the snow.

The rest of the team flung themselves into a furry, writhing pile. The fact that the prey had escaped didn't deter the dogs. They loved any excuse for a good fight.

Rebecca's dad had sprinted up the line of dogs to reach Apollo and now waded into the pile.

Rebecca wanted to grab at the back tug lines and help break the dogs apart, but she stood frozen in place.

"H-h-how's Apollo?" her voice squeaked out. "Is he okay?" *Those sharp teeth can chew through trees.* Her throat closed in horror. *Is he gonna lose his leg?*

"Dad? Is Apollo okay?" Rebecca found her voice and screamed over the noise of the dogs.

"He's fine, Becca." Her dad struggled to straighten out the team. "Sacre bleu ... Apollo, that's enough!"

Rebecca watched as her dad finally separated the dogs. He unhooked Apollo and carried him back to the sled. Blaze leaned into her harness, holding the team out. *She's such a good lead dog.*

"How are you to drive?" her dad asked, breathing heavy. Apollo thrashed in his arms. Deep red blood splattered across the snow.

Drive? Rebecca's mind reeled with images of flying uncontrolled down a hill. Or flipping over around a corner, crashing into trees, dogs tangled, Apollo shrieking ...

Rebecca tried to steady her voice, "Okay."

Her dad climbed into the sled with Apollo. "Just stand on the brake there ... make sure you've got the brake before you pull the hook."

Rebecca's mouth went dry. She chewed her bottom lip and reached for the sled with a shaky hand. "I know, I know. I've watched you a million times." *Just stand on the brake ... stand on the brake.*

She did not want her dad to know how her legs felt like cooked spaghetti. How a big rock sat in her gut. She wanted to show him she was old enough to drive the team now without him standing behind her on the runners.

With both feet on the brake, Rebecca bent down and yanked the heavy claw hook out of the snow. When the team lurched forward, she nearly fell backward, but the brake slowed them enough for her to gain balance. She hung the hook on the back of the sled, tightened her grip around the wooden handlebar, and stood straight.

The surge of power from seven dogs pulling rushed up through her feet and rumbled in the handlebar. Her legs braced on every bump. A hot thrill raced through her blood as she dared to glance around. She stood, in control of her own dog team, sprinting down a narrow trail. Her lips pressed tightly together, the dimple in her cheek deepening as her mouth turned up at the corners.

When the dogs slowed from a gallop to their usual racing trot, Rebecca's death-grip began to relax. She let out a breath she didn't know she'd been holding. Her skin tingled with excitement.

Rebecca watched Blaze carefully and when she slowed, toed the brake to tighten the slack in the gang line for her. The dogs ran behind Blaze, two-by-two in a line. As she ran, Blaze threw a quick glance over her shoulder at Rebecca. Their eyes connected for a moment.

She's counting on me. We're in this together. Rebecca stood a little straighter. *I won't let you down.*

Vapor from the dogs' breath puffed out behind them. Rebecca exhaled to make her own puff. She could almost believe she was part of a wolf pack out for a run. The dogs padded across the snow, tongues out, ears forward, focused on the next bend in the trail. Rebecca breathed in the fresh scent in the wind. Listened to the "shush" of the runners, the tinkling of the metal clips on the neck lines. She felt each movement of the dogs like an extension of herself.

"How're you doing?" her dad asked, interrupting her daydream. He tried to look behind him, but struggled with Apollo. The gangly dog complained with a blast of growling whines. He didn't seem to like the fact he wasn't leading the team. Apollo stretched his neck and arched his back against the long arms around him. Rebecca noticed Apollo's alert, focused expression.

That has to be a good sign. Apollo will be okay, won't he? The knot twitched a little in her stomach.

"Don't worry, Dad, I've got it." And with a thrill of relief, she realized she really did. The dogs knew this trail and usually loved these last few kilometers. It would be easy going back to the dog yard – except for the last corner. Rebecca avoided thinking about the boomerang-shaped corner of doom at the bottom of the last steep hill.

She rode the runners, watched the team, and pretended to be Susan Butcher. Rebecca considered how her Iditarod-winning hero looked in the poster on her bedroom wall. She had stared at the poster before falling asleep for so long, she had it memorized. She thought she even looked the same as Susan. Fur hat? Check. Dog team? Check. Big smile on her face? Check, check.

Maybe I really can be like Susan Butcher and run an actual race. Alone on the trail … with my own team. Yeah. I can do that. And I'll be the best twelve-year-old musher the world has ever seen. I'll dazzle them all. People will call my name — Rebecca Bourdon, Pro Musher. I should start practicing signing my name for autographs. A smile, just a tiny bit smug, played on her lips.

Her smile faded when they reached the top of the last hill. Her stomach squeezed as she peered down the abyss.

"Keep ready on the brake," her dad said. "And lean on the inside runner … don't forget to lean."

The sled barreled over the crest of the hill. They dropped over the ridge and Rebecca's guts twisted upside down. The dogs ran low to the ground. Rebecca clutched the cold handlebar so hard, her forearms cramped. She forced her eyes wide open.

Don't crash, don't crash, don't crash.

Chapter Two

They sped down the hill with the two metal tips of the brake carving deep lines into the trail. Snow spray flew behind them. They reached the corner faster than Rebecca expected. She shifted her weight like a downhill skier, and pulled on the handlebar. They careened around the curve and wobbled slightly on one runner. Rebecca fumbled with her grip, and corrected herself by leaning out to the side even farther. She instinctively dropped her center of gravity and stuck out her bent knee for balance. The sled skidded sideways with an impressive "sshh".

The team pounded down the last stretch of trail and after one more little bump, they slid flawlessly into the yard. Rebecca jumped on the brake with both feet.

"Whoa, Blaze." Rebecca panted as hard as the

dogs. Her heart thumped in her ears. *Pro-musher Bourdon has done it, folks. The crowds are going nuts — she's managed to bring home all the dogs with style, and survived the Corner of Doom.* A beaming smile shone on her hot face.

She planted the snow hook and gave it a kick into the snow, like her dad always did. Rebecca felt the steel of the hook through her new mukluks. She noticed how much lighter they were than her regular boots with the hard soles. It felt like wearing warm slippers in the snow.

"Well done, Becca." Her dad's long legs unfolded out of the sled and he bent to pick up Apollo. "Can you get the — "

"Yeah, I've got the team, Dad. No worries. Just go call the vet."

"Thanks, Hon. You're the best."

Rebecca grinned and nodded. *The sled handling skills displayed in that ride — just mind-blowing, folks. Keep watch for this rising star.*

She started unhooking the dogs at the back of the team. The wheel dogs, the strongest pullers, were closest to the sled. Denali stood with his tongue hanging out the side of his wide grin. The rest of the team rolled in the snow, grabbing big mouthfuls, splaying their legs with bellies pressed against the coolness.

"Yo, Denali." Rebecca grabbed the leash off the post, clipped it to his collar and rubbed his wide head. "You did good today. Yes, you did. You're a good dog."

Denali ignored her. He stared intently toward the puppy pen just a few steps away from where the team had stopped. Rebecca's arm threatened to pop out of its socket as the dog dug in and furiously scrabbled forward.

"Okay, okay. Frig."

Denali jumped up on the door of the pen and peered over the top. Rebecca looked up at him as he stood on his back feet. His granite-gray bulk quivered in eagerness. He whined at the four, chubby, two-month-old pups inside the pen.

"Hey, git off the door, dummy, I can't open it." Rebecca pushed Denali off with her shoulder and opened the pen. The pups exploded out and attacked Denali like ants climbing up a piece of watermelon. He flopped on his back and let them grab his ears with their sharp puppy teeth.

"Big tough Denali." Rebecca giggled. "Okay, that's enough." She steered Denali past the pen toward the dog yard, and snickered at the ruckus the pups were causing among the team behind her. She clipped Denali to his spot. He padded to his doghouse, a wooden box full of straw with a rim around the doorway. He cocked his back leg on the corner of it where a gruesome, yellowish ice sculpture glistened.

"Yup, that's your house." She wrinkled her nose

at the evidence of Denali's regular marking habit, but gave him a hug.

The pups had found their mother. Elsie watched Rebecca's approach with resigned eyes as she stood with a pup dangling from each ear like a pair of earrings.

Rebecca snickered at her, and then reached for Tarzan. He pulled his lips back as she clapped him on the shoulder. His mouthful of teeth starkly contrasted with his black face. Rebecca grimaced back at him and then laughed. His tail wagged so hard his whole butt swayed as he flashed evil looking canines.

"Zany, you're never gonna get people to love you back if you keep looking like you'll gnaw off their legs." Rebecca didn't know why Tarzan smiled like a person, but she loved that he did.

One by one, Rebecca spent time with each dog until only the leader remained. "Blaze." Rebecca almost whispered the name as she knelt in the snow. She saw Blaze differently now, after their intense run together. Rebecca's brown eyes glittered with the memory of their recent adventure. Blaze rolled on her back with her legs out.

"What do you think about us running a race?" Rebecca asked, as she rubbed a mitten against Blaze's pink belly. As Blaze returned her look, it semmed to Rebecca she was saying, *Becca, you'll be fabulous in a race.*

Rebecca's grin turned into a grimace as she thought about actually racing. It was fun to think about the finish line and how famous she'd be. But when her mind played out the start of a race, her stomach tightened. And then there was the middle of the race. Her teeth clamped on her bottom lip.

"What if we get lost Blaze? All by ourselves … at night … in the dark. What if we can't find the right trail?"

Blaze pawed the air with her front feet and stretched her back legs out further. *Let's go!* Blaze appeared to say.

Rebecca shook her head as if to clear away her fearful thoughts. "First problem we face is getting Dad to let us."

They beelined to the dog yard, and the pups left a wide berth around the dominant lead dog. They knew which dogs they could climb on.

Rebecca secured Blaze, and then bent to scoop up Doppler, her favorite puppy. She ran toward her house, a log home made with red pines stained brown, and a blue tin roof. She felt like the Pied Piper with the other three pups following behind.

Doppler sat like an overstuffed hamster in her arms. Large black spots scattered across his white fur. One black spot centered perfectly around his left eye. His soft brown eyes studied Rebecca's face. She pulled off her mitt and grabbed a front paw as it dangled in the air with each bounce of her step. His pads felt warm and thick.

"You have really big feet, Mister." Rebecca rolled him on his back and clucked her tongue at how lazy he looked with his belly hanging out. "How're you gonna grow up to be a good sled dog when you're such a suck? Your dad's an awesome leader ... but he got into trouble today."

Rebecca's brow creased as she recalled the horrible image of Apollo's leg bleeding on the snow. *They'll be half an hour driving in to Thunder Bay. Won't be home till supper. I'd better get the dog food soaking.*

Rebecca held the door open for the pups, who struggled up the stone steps. She felt the warm air from the woodstove spill out the open door. She put Doppler down, went to the mud room, and turned on the hot water tap over the feed bucket. As it filled, she took off her hat and goggles and peeled off her anorak. Three of the pups rumbled through the room on a seek-and-destroy mission but Doppler sat by Rebecca's feet and watched her.

"Are you worried, too?" she asked him as she turned off the water and picked up the axe handle they used for stirring. A familiar smell wafted up. Chicken fat and ground meat, cooked rice, commercial dog food, and warm water. *Smells sort of like chicken stew.*

She turned her head to a thump behind her. "Minden, drop that!" She wrestled her stepmom's leather boot from the vicious attack of puppy teeth, and then paused, holding the boot in the air. A little smile flickered across Rebecca's face and she tossed the boot back to Minden. She skipped into the living room.

Rebecca flopped onto the soft plaid couch and a poof of white dog hair floated to the floor. She let Doppler stalk her socks. *The Dad problem needs to be solved. How to prove I'm ready? Well, I drove the team by myself today. That has to count. And I just did chores without being asked. Maybe if I do more things on my own, Dad will see I can handle racing.*

Her thoughts strayed to the Thunder Dog sled dog race that her dad entered last year. She imagined herself walking to the podium at the mushers' meeting, reaching into the hat to draw her start number, receiving her racing bib. The side of Rebecca's mouth twitched up. *A race bib. When I wear my number, everyone will see I'm a musher — not just a handler anymore. They'll see I train my own team. They might even ask me for training tips.*

She watched Doppler absently as he climb over her knees. Then the obvious answer popped into her head. She sat up. *Of course — I'll train the pups!*

The phone rang. Her heart tripped. *Apollo.*

Chapter Three

"**H**ey, Ribby. Whatcha doin'?"

"Oh, Jackie, I can't talk now. My dad's about to call, I think."

As usual, Jackie continued without seeming to hear her. "Well, my mom wanted to ask if you guys could give rides at the Winter Carnival. She's on the committee and I think she promised 'em somethin' special. Not that your mutts are special."

"I don't know … Apollo's at the vet right now and it looks bad." Rebecca ignored the dig at her dogs. She was used to it from Jackie.

"The ugly one?"

"He got attacked by a beaver! Then, I drove them back. By myself. There was blood on the snow. A lot. And screaming …" Rebecca's voice caught as she re-lived the scene. She took a deep breath and swallowed. *Maybe Dad's trying to call right now*. "I gotta go."

"Crap. A beaver? I want to hear all about it to-morrow on the bus."

Rebecca hung up and jumped to save the lamp cord. "No, Minden. Drop that."

The phone rang again, and she immediately re-laxed when she heard her dad's chipper voice.

"We're finally on our way home. Apollo's been made into a hat so we don't have to worry about him anymore."

"Yeah, Dad, you're hilarious. He's okay?"

"Yup, he makes a very handsome hat ... with black earflaps ..."

"Dad!"

"He's okay, Becca. Can you make some Kraft Dinner or something? I'm starving."

Rebecca felt a lightness in her chest. She hadn't been this worried about a dog since last month when Blaze mysteriously got loose and didn't come home for two days. She had the same knot in her stomach then, and felt the same sense of relief now as when Blaze appeared at breakfast as if she hadn't left. Rebecca felt like celebrating.

She put on her favorite Pussy Cat Dolls CD and turned it up. When she was old enough, she wanted to audition for Canadian Idol. If they came to Thunder Bay, she planned on being prepared.

Doppler cocked his head as she danced across the hardwood floor. Rebecca used a wooden spoon as a microphone and watched her reflection in the picture windows. She pulled off her scrunchie and tossed her long brown hair over her shoulder. "Careful what you wish for 'cause you just might get it …"

Lead singer, Rebecca Bourdon just invented another signature move folks — and she's doing it in her blue, polka-dotted long johns. She turned around and wiggled her butt. *At least they don't have a trap door.*

Rebecca was so engrossed in the song, she forgot about the puppies. Until she heard a loud bang coming from her dad's bedroom. Rebecca's head snapped around.

Uh-oh.

She raced toward the noise, still holding the wooden spoon. She noticed her dad's normally closed door ajar, and peeked her head in. When she heard another crash from the bathroom, she dashed into the room. Rebecca reached the door, swung it open, and slapped on the light. She sucked in her breath.

"Oh, no!" Rebecca dropped the spoon and covered her eyes with her hands. She peeked through her fingers and cringed.

Doppler and the three little imps blinked up at her from the center of the apparent bombing. Then they turned to continue their fun. The toilet paper roll, obviously one that held reams of paper, hung limply on the wall with one sheet. The entire room looked as if a big bag of blizzard had hit it. Tiny shredded toilet paper pieces hung in the snow-globed air. A piece fluttered onto her foot. The rest decorated the shower stall, the toilet, every inch of the floor, and the puppies. Doppler grinned at Rebecca with a blue-tinged face.

What the ...?

A jar of bath salts lay on the floor, its lid popped off and crystals spilling out like a blue tongue.

Oh.

Magazines lay shredded in various stages of slaughter, poking out from under the knocked over shelves. A stainless steel waste basket lay on its side, the entire contents pulled out and chewed into a million pieces.

Tenacious little growls turned Rebecca's attention to the tug-of-war with a white towel.

"Frig!" She bent, pried the towel away, and placed it back on the rack. "Dad is going to *kill* us!" *So much for training the pups.*

Rebecca sprung into action erasing the evidence before anyone else could see. All the while, she listened intently for her dad coming home. She ran back to the living room to shut off the music, and saw a beam of light shine across the kitchen wall. A chorus of howls erupted outside. She raced back to the bathroom, righted the shelf, and collected the magazine pieces. Her gaze swept the room one last time. With her heart thumping, she buried the magazines in the kitchen garbage. She flicked on the dog yard flood lights and saw Tarzan standing on his house with his muzzle straight up.

"Oooooow."

The pups ran to the door. She let them out and they scampered down the stairs. At the bottom, they joined in the song. Their high voices totally out of tune and louder than any of the adults. They almost drowned out the noise of the truck turning around in the driveway.

"How is he?" Rebecca called innocently from the doorway. She shivered in the chilled air and remembered she hadn't even changed clothes yet.

"Be good as new in a week or so." Apollo towed her dad on a leash as the dog scrabbled for the house. "Vet said it's a simple puncture … didn't hit anything serious."

"Well, he looks good," Rebecca said with a laugh. "Hey, you gonna watch out for beavers now?" She stroked Apollo's black head as he pushed past her. The only evidence of his ordeal was the purple vet-wrap around his leg.

"We'll keep him in tonight, to watch him. Did you get the food soaking?"

"Yup, all set."

After they fed the dogs, Rebecca's dad sat at the table reading the newspaper while she stirred the macaroni with green peas to make it healthy.

"Mrs. Gower wants to know if you can give

rides at the Winter Carnival."

"When is it?"

Rebecca ladled the pasta into two bowls. "I dunno. I forgot to ask."

"We'll need Apollo for that, but if he's back in shape, I suppose we could." Her dad walked to the sink with his relaxed, long-legged gait, and ducked under the pine beam with a practiced tilt of his head. He washed the newsprint off his hands, whistling loudly as he did.

"Do you think maybe … I dunno, maybe I could … like …"

"Spit it out."

"Could I, like, help you give rides?"

Her dad scooted his chair up to the table. "If it happens, I'll need some help, yes."

"Yeah, but, I mean … can I be the one to *give* the rides? Like drive the team?"

Without a response her dad resumed eating. Rebecca tried to look at him out of the corner of her eye. Her hair draped between them like a curtain. She felt a tremor in her stomach at the thought of giving rides on her own, to people she didn't even know. But she set her mouth in a determined line. *It's Step One of my new plan. The famous-dogsled-racer plan.*

She kept her slightly tanned face perfectly void of expression. *Poker face, poker face. If he says no, I may have to flash the dimple. Parental manipulation. Sac-*

rifice my pride for the good of the team.

Her dad sat back, wiping his mustache with a napkin. "How about we sleep on that." He took the dishes to the kitchen. "And how about you use that spectacular imagination of yours and imagine yourself doing your homework."

Probably should've used the dimple.

Rebecca sat at her desk and tried to concentrate on her times tables. She tapped her pencil on her teeth. She sighed. She drew a dog paw on the margin of the page. She sighed again and looked up at the poster of Susan and her dogs.

Rebecca's room didn't have the Teen Beat posters plastered all over the walls like Jackie's. In fact, her rounded log walls didn't look anything like Jackie's pink walls with white trim. Rebecca rubbed her hand absently across the wood. Her walls felt warm and alive, they matched the area rug on the floor with its funky blue and red splashes.

Out of habit, Rebecca reached for the glass bottle that had sat on her desk since she was seven. CANADA'S WONDERLAND was stamped in red into the bottom wood frame. A tiny replica of the pirate ship ride sat inside the bottle. She ran her fingers over the familiar souvenir. She thought of that day the three of them had ridden the ship. A family. If she stared at it long enough, perhaps she could finally catch that feeling again. Catch the laughter like a delicate dandelion seed blowing in a summer wind. Catch that one whole day when no one argued about dogs.

Rebecca shook her head and set the bottle down. She stabbed her pencil through one of the three holes along the side of her page and spun it around. *No one at school's gonna understand why I want to run a race — especially Jackie.* Rebecca slapped the page down and stood to re-arrange her ceramic frog collection on the shelf above her desk.

Why do I want to race? Why can't I be normal like everyone else in my class? Hang at the curling club on weekends. Maybe have one pet dog and a gecko. She glanced again at the poster, and ran her gaze over the dogs' shining eyes, flashing teeth, frosted fur, and abruptly recalled the delicious thrill of mushing the team.

She smiled.

Sled dogs or gecko, not much of a competition there. Whether or not Jackie told her she was weird, she would do it anyway.

Rebecca sat and grabbed her paper again. She wrote, PLAN FOR FAME across the top. She was so busy scribbling down notes that she jumped when she heard her dad call up. *Time for bed and math not even started. Whoever said "fame costs" was right. I'm gonna have to do this on the bus.*

Rebecca padded in to the living room wearing

her red flannel pajamas with dog prints. She saw that her stepmom, Heather, was home from work and automatically frowned.

"Bonne nuit," her dad said, looking up from his book. "Mon petit chou."

"Bonne nuit," Rebecca said. She rolled her eyes at their nightly French game. Her dad had said, 'good night my little cabbage,' to her every night since she could remember.

She looked for an excuse to stay, in case her dad wanted to finish their earlier conversation.

"Night, Apollo."

Apollo lounged on the couch across Heather's lap with his four feet sticking up in the air. Rebecca kissed the top of his head.

"G'night, Rebecca," Heather said. She appeared squashed under the big dog, her round face smiling behind his feet.

Rebecca nodded.

"Don't forget …" her dad began.

"About?"

"To let your teacher know you'll be skipping Friday. You still want to help me bring the pups to the kindergarten classes?"

"Oh, yeah. Right."

"Oh, and Heather," her dad sat up. "Have you seen the new issue of Mushing Magazine?"

Think that's my cue to leave.

Chapter Four

After school, Rebecca hopped off the bus, dropped her pack on the front steps and hurried to the dog yard.

"Hey, Becca." Her dad strode toward her carrying the pooper-scooper. Rebecca stopped for a shocked moment at the sight of her dad doing her chores. He was usually still inside writing when she came home. His latest book seemed to be taking him extra long. *What's going on?*

"I got a call from Mrs. Gower today. We'll be giving rides at the carnival next weekend." He leaned the scooper on the side of the shed.

"Is Apollo gonna be okay by then?" Rebecca saw the dog moving with ease in his circle.

"Should be. But, he still can't run with us for a few days, at least."

Rebecca noticed then the two sleds sitting at

the trailhead. "So ... have you thought about me running the team yet?"

"I think you'll have to start training if you're going to be ready in two weeks." Her dad laughed at the excited sparkle in her eyes. "We'll try these teams today." He handed Rebecca a slip of paper with dogs names listed in the positions they would be running.

Blaze   Tarzan Soho
Jade Nitro   Denali
        Elsie

"This is my team?" Rebecca pointed to the three-dog team.

Her dad nodded. "Any problems?" He glanced at her sideways and seemed to be testing to make sure she was really ready.

"No. No. Got it." Rebecca's face remained calm, but her guts twisted with excitement and terror in equal measures. *What if I fall off around a corner? What if I can't hold Denali? What if we have another beaver episode?* She shook herself and forced a deep breath. *Don't forget the plan. Phase one of the plan doesn't include having a seizure at the thought of running my own team.*

"You'll have lots of power since you're the chase team. Zany should be fine up front, but I'd watch Soho. If she acts up, put her with Denali. They can run in wheel together."

"Acts up?"

"Yeah, I'm not sure if she'll lead. If she sticks up her tail you'll know she's not pulling. You should switch her if she does that or starts looking around. And watch her ears too, they should point forward, and swivel back if you say something." Her dad studied her face. "If she's not happy up there, she'll let you know."

"Right, right." Rebecca swallowed. She couldn't stop her grin. Her dad was finally letting her do this on her own. *I'm gonna make sure Soho stays happy.*

"Go get your gear on. I'll put the pups away and get the harnesses."

Rebecca raced to the house and threw on a pair of snow pants over her jeans.

Mitts and toques flew out of the bin while she tried to find her goggles.

Once ready, she joined her dad who stood in the shed scratching his head.

"Where did you put the harnesses, Bec?"

"I always hang them right here, where they belong." She pointed to an empty hook on the wall.

"Hmm. That's odd." Her dad scanned the shed, gave a slight shrug, and then opened a metal cabinet. He pulled out a pile of spare harnesses.

"These will do for now." He handed her three.

"I've got the gang lines laid out and the sleds are tied to the trees with their snubs. We'll do the inside route today. A short ten k for your first time. Sound good?"

"Yup." Rebecca held up a large blue harness. "This one's for Denali?"

"Yeah, but put the leaders out first …"

"I know."

"And what's the most important rule?"

"Never let go of the sled," Rebecca chanted the familiar phrase.

They both grabbed a leash off the post and walked toward the yard. The dogs, who had been watching their every move, suddenly erupted in frantic, high-pitched screams, bawling to be first.

Each dog had worn a path in a perfect circle around a rotating car axle driven into the ground. Their ten foot chains attached to the axles and allowed them to socialize and play with the dogs around them. Every dog tore around his circle, exchanging insults with his neighbors

The chaos of hook-up always made Rebecca nervous. Her mouth turned down as she spastically tried to stick the harness over Tarzan's head. He leaped up and foamy goobs flew out of his mouth onto Rebecca's sleeve. Her nerves jangled from the noise and urgency in the air. She glanced at her dad and saw him doing it properly, straddling Blaze.

Get a grip Rebecca. You know how to do this. She straddled Tarzan, forcing him to stay down as she slipped the harness over his head. She hardly had to grab his feet before he punched his legs through the harness for her.

They skirted around Apollo's circle to get to the sled. This seemed to offend the dominant dog. His indignant barks sounded like, *Now, now, NOW!*

Tarzan dug in, dragging her toward the sled.

She attached the back of Tarzan's harness to the tug line and left him to get the next dog. He raked the ground with outstretched claws, and screamed at the team ahead.

When Rebecca passed Apollo's circle again, his furious gaze fixed on her, commanding her to pick him next. His hooked foot snaked out and caught Rebecca's leg, pulling her toward him.

"Apollo ... sheesh. Sorry, but you can't come." Rebecca tried to hide her smile. She didn't want him to think she was laughing at the psychotic gleam in his eyes.

Rebecca secured the rest of her team without mishap. Her dad glanced back to see if she was ready, then pulled his snub line, and disappeared down the trail.

Rebecca stood on the runners of her bouncing, straining sled. When she imagined her first time alone, she thought there'd be more dogs. She

imagined a long string of them cruising effortlessly along a gleaming white trail. Spruce, heavy
with snow, sparkled in the sun. In her visions, she
could feel her dogs like an invisible cord attached
them to her. In her visions, her legs felt solid and
her hands definitely did not shake.

*Driving a smaller team will be easier to control than
our last run. Yeah, probably better.*

Her dogs watched the team ahead take off. It
drove her team into a frenzy. They howled. They
clawed the air. Rebecca reached for the snub. She
yanked the slip-knot loose.

Instant silence.

The dogs launched after the other team, intent
on the chase. Rebecca gripped the handlebar like
a skydiver would grip his ripcord. Cold air rushed
into her wide-open eyes. She had forgotten to pull
her goggles down from her forehead, but now
it was too risky to let go of the sled. They raced
around a bend in the trail, trying to catch her dad's
team. Rebecca dug in with the inside runner and
skied around the corner.

Chunks of ice flew off the dogs' feet and
bounced on Rebecca's chest. Sometimes, more
than just ice flew back. The dogs were trained to
poop while they ran, as all racing sled dogs are.
Rebecca kept watch for brown missiles flying in
her direction. She made sure to close her mouth.

The frantic sprint lasted a few kilometers, then

they fell into an easy pace. Rebecca's dad glanced back. She gave him a thumbs-up with her big mitten, and then wiped at the tears forming at the corners of her eyes from the wind. A bare branch hung low over the trail. Rebecca ducked as they sped past. *Super-pro Bourdon, dodges obstacles like a young Susan Butcher. She's incredible, folks.*

She watched Soho's ears flicking forward. Tarzan's tug line snapped tightly behind him. He would help to keep Soho in line. As Rebecca admired her leaders, she could already hear the wild applause from the audience when she raced across the finish line. *Maybe they'll make a bronze statue of me and Tarzan like the one of Balto.*

Another corner brought her attention back.

"Zany, we'd better start practicing our smiles." Rebecca's delighted grin grew wider as she rounded the corner with a little flourish of snow. She thought again about training the pups. If she could handle three adults careening down a narrow trail, she could deal with four little puppies. *On Friday, I'll show Dad when we tour the kindergarten classes. Everyone will be dazzled by my puppy handling skills. What could go wrong in a kindergarten class?*

Chapter Five

"**C**rap, it's not fair," Jackie said, after school. Her glossy lips pulled down in a pout. "I wish *I* could skip school tomorrow to help with a bunch of puppies."

"You don't even like puppies," Rebecca reminded her. She lifted an eyebrow at her friend, then settled farther down in the bus seat with her knees folded against the bench in front of them. "It's gonna be fun. Dad said when they went last week, Doppler peed on the floor, and all the kids screamed like it was a toxic flood."

"Ew! Gag-o-rama." Jackie flipped her blonde hair off her shoulder with a practiced flick. "Are you bringing your freaky dog too ... Zohan or Zeenon, whatever his name is?" Her blue eyes, highlighted with powder-blue eye shadow, sparkled as she teased.

"You know it's Zany, Jackie. Sheesh. And no, he's not coming, we're just socializing the pups. It's good for them to get poked and handled, makes them better sled dogs when they grow up."

"So, you think you'll get to drive the team at the crap-tastic Carnival?"

"Yeah, I'm pretty sure Dad's gonna let me. Apollo is better already, but he's still not running." Rebecca's gaze became unfocused as she imagined she was back behind the team. "You should see him. He gets so mad when we take the teams out."

"Earth to Ribby ... hello? Can you not visit your home planet when I'm sitting right in front of you?" Jackie reached for the wayward hair, that always escaped Rebecca's pony-tail, and tucked it behind her ear. She snapped her gum and flashed her devil grin. "I hope Chris and Scott are going to the carnival. Did you see Scott's face in life skills class when they showed the *reproduction* movie?"

Rebecca sighed as Jackie launched into the twenty-seventh retelling of how Scott raised his eyebrows up and down in her friend's direction. *He probably had something in his eye.* Rebecca nodded and tried to show interest. She knew Jackie didn't care about her adventures with the dogs. But she didn't understand why not. *How can anyone not like dogs? Well, I guess I can think of one other person. But Mom could still change her mind.*

Rebecca steadied herself with the belief that

her mom would soon get tired of being a lawyer in Toronto. She'd come back and live with them again. But last year her dad went and married Heather. That complicated matters. *If she would just leave, Mom could come home and everything would be the way it used to.*

The bus slowed, and Jackie gathered her books. "You should let me put make-up on you for the carnival, Ribby."

"Bye, Jackie, have fun at school tomorrow." Rebecca gave a cheeky grin as she waved. *Seriously, we've known each other since grade one. You'd think she'd know by now that famous mushers do not wear make-up.*

The bus turned off the highway at the rock cut with ribbons of gneiss layered in the granite like a pink snake. It towered above the windows and gleamed in the setting sun. Rebecca bounced as the bus rolled along her dead-end road. She stared out her window at the wall of aspen and pines. Sometimes deer darted out in front of vehicles. With only two houses on the road, the area attracted a wide variety of wildlife.

"Hey!" A thin girl wearing a brown corduroy skirt plopped down next to Rebecca. "So … how're the dogs?"

Rebecca smiled at her neighbor, "Oh, hi Robin. The dogs are good." Rebecca's gaze dropped to their laps. Her own knees looked thick compared to Robin's clad in black leotard.

For the last five minutes on the bus, only the two of them were left. Robin and her mom had moved in last year, but she still didn't have many friends at school. Rebecca talked with her at first because she felt bad for her. But she soon discovered that Robin was very interested in the dogs. Rebecca liked having someone to talk dog with.

"Can I come over again tonight to see the puppies?" Robin pushed her glasses up her nose with a knuckle.

"Um … we're busy with them right now." Rebecca felt a twinge of guilt as Robin's smile dropped. "How 'bout this weekend?"

"You getting off, Hon?" The driver peered at Rebecca in the rear view mirror.

"Oh, yeah." She grabbed her things and bolted off the bus to the usual sound of the dogs singing her a welcome.

The next morning, Rebecca trundled out to feed and water the dogs. She stopped when she saw the puppy pen door wide open. Her heart beat faster. *Did I forget to close the door? Has it been open all night? Are the pups gone?* She thought she had secured the latch just like every night after chores.

Doppler heard her approach, and poked his head out of the dog house he shared with his litter mates. Rebecca's breath escaped in a rush. Her brows furrowed together as she imagined what dire ways the pups could have been killed. Wild animals, traffic, lost in the bush …

   She knelt down when the puppies charged toward her. A mix of doubt, relief, and fear swept through her leaving her slightly sick. It reminded her of when Blaze disappeared. The whole time the dog was missing, Rebecca tortured herself wondering if she had somehow failed to secure her properly. She still wondered.

   She would not tell anyone about the pen door.

Chapter Six

After chores and breakfast, Rebecca gathered the pups for their big day at the east end public schools. She felt a little disappointed they weren't going to her own school, but this way, if she said something dumb, no one would know her.

The dog truck had eight separate wooden boxes built into it, one for each dog. They all had their own metal-screened door with a latch, and a layer of straw for bedding. The dogs liked to stick their noses through the wire. Rebecca had painted their names above the doors using a stencil.

While Rebecca stuffed two pups into one box, Doppler bounced at her feet waiting for his turn. He already knew that going for a ride in the big truck meant going someplace fun.

Rebecca put Doppler into a box with Minden, and jumped into the front seat. "That's all of 'em."

As they arrived at the school, promptly at ten AM, Rebecca's dad gave her a wink as they parked. "We'll leave them in the truck until we're ready for them," he said.

A teacher sauntered over to the truck and peered into the boxes as they gathered their things. "What do you have in here? Chickens?"

"Dogs," Rebecca said. *Everyone always asks the same questions.*

"Dogs? The boxes are so small."

"It's like a seat belt for them," Rebecca said.

"Hey little dogs. Mush! Heh, heh." The teacher started to poke a finger in to the box, hesitated, then dropped his hand.

"Uh, mushers don't actually say mush to the dogs — only in bad movies." *Nerd alert, he doesn't know much for a teacher.*

"We have to get going or we'll be late for class," her dad said.

Rebecca thought she saw a satisfied smile on her dad's face as they walked toward the school. She smiled secretly in her head.

When they were introduced by Mrs. Andress, the class's beaming teacher, Rebecca scanned the sea of shiny five-year-old faces. They bounced and fidgeted as they sat on the floor, staring up at her. One had a finger up her nose, another had his hands down his pants. Rebecca traced the floor pattern with her toe. She didn't know there would be so many kids.

Her dad told stories about their life with the dogs while Rebecca passed around dog gear for everyone to touch.

Finally, her dad said, "Okay, who wants to meet some future sled dogs?"

Shrieks echoed around the room and arms shot up high. To the kids' delight, Rebecca's dad picked up several boys and pretended they were puppies as he organized the class in a circle. "Rebecca, can you go get them now?"

Rebecca ran outside and peeked in on Doppler. "Are you guys awake?"

The pups slept together in a ball, but Doppler raised his head when he heard Rebecca's voice. She opened the door and reached in. An earthy, comforting smell of fresh straw and puppies drifted out. The small box held the body heat, so when she pulled Minden out, she squirmed and yawned in protest.

Ah, puppy breath. She hooked her left arm under Minden and Doppler's arms, leaving their bottom halves to hang down her chest. With her free arm, she grabbed the other two and waddled toward the school. Eight puppy feet dangled to her waist.

At the closed door, she mentally chided herself for not propping it open with a stone or something. Rebecca balanced on one leg and toed the door handle. The pups' weight shifted and she teetered, frantically juggling her load like sacks of flour. Suddenly, the door opened and a passing teacher smiled at her. "Wow, you've got quite a handful there."

"Thank you! They just woke up so they're not moving much."

When Rebecca appeared at the door of the classroom, squeals of delight broke out.

"Aaaww! I want to hold them."

"Are they heavy?"

"Do they bite?"

"Let me touch!"

Rebecca put them all on the floor in the middle of the circle. For a quiet moment, no one moved. And then Doppler padded over to a chubby blonde girl with pig-tails and licked her fingers. Rebecca smiled with pride.

"Tickles!" the girl squealed.

Rebecca's dad leaned over, and ran his fingers against Doppler's fur. "You can see they have fur like a wolf." He rubbed from the tail to the head. "Feel the thick undercoat here. See how soft it is? This keeps them warm so they can stay outside."

The girl ran her fingers inside Doppler's lush coat. Her eyes closed briefly at the pleasure of the downy fur.

"And these guys are just developing their coarse outer-hair, called guard hairs. It repels water and protects the undercoat." Her dad rubbed the top of Doppler's back. The other puppies began to roam around the circle, and the kids reached their small hands out to touch the coats.

A cell phone rang, and Rebecca's dad reached into his pocket. After a moment he pressed the phone to his chest.

"Rebecca, can you take over? This is important." He brought the phone back to his ear as he walked out. "Yeah, Davis, I've got a minute. What's wrong with the copy edits?"

Rebecca's face paled as her gaze darted between all the kids watching her expectantly. She cleared her throat. As she leaned over the girl with pig-tails, she turned over one of Doppler's feet.

"See ... see his good feet," she said. The girl watched Rebecca with baby-owl eyes. It helped Rebecca's nerves. *This is exactly what I need to show Dad I'm ready to race. I can teach a class. By myself!*

She spoke louder, "We look for tough feet. Feel his pads? We don't like long fur between his toes either, that collects snowballs and ..."

Rebecca broke off when she noticed Minden making a break for it between two shy children. Fully awake now, and brimming with wild joy, the rest of the pups saw an opportunity. Before anyone could stop them, they dashed through the hole in the living fence. Doppler leaped off Pigtail's lap and joined in the fun. Gleeful laughter broke out around the classroom. The pups darted under chairs, through legs, avoiding capture by Mrs. Andress. Doppler rumbled to the classroom door and nosed it open. All four of them scampered out into the hallways. The puppies sounded like a tribe of monkeys escaping from the zoo.

No! This can't be happening.

The class cheered. They raced to the door, pushing and elbowing each other. Rebecca heard a muffled, galloping chase and charged into the hall after the pups. They raced ahead, sliding on the smooth floor, and bouncing off the walls like pin balls. Minden squatted and peed just as Mrs. Andress made a running lunge at her. The teacher slipped in the puddle. Both feet scooted out from under her, one of her shoes flew off, and she crashed down with a smack.

Several kids from the class had spilled into the halls, and collapsed into hysterics at the site of Mrs. Andress on the floor. One girl pumped her legs on the spot, like she was running a marathon. Another let loose a piercing, un-ending shriek that sounded like an abandoned kettle.

Minden slipped between Rebecca's legs and chased Doppler through a partially open classroom door. The rest of the pups trooped into the room behind them. Rebecca clapped her hands over her mouth to contain the mix of horror and a fit of giggles that threatened to escape.

Should I go into the classroom?

Just as the chair scuffling and shrieking began, Rebecca's dad rushed past her and barged into the room. If a circus truck crashed into the school and its entire menagerie of animals spilled out, there would have been less ruckus than what came from that classroom.

Moments later, her dad returned to the doorway. He had a dark look on his face, and four squirming pups in his arms. He shot an irritated glance at Rebecca

"Well, I think this is a good time to wrap up," he said to Mrs. Andress. "I apologize. That was the first time that's happened."

"That was certainly interesting," Mrs. Andress said as she smoothed out her pant suit. Stray hairs stuck to the dampness on her forehead, and she pushed them off her reddened face. "Everybody thank Mr. Bourdon and Rebecca."

Rebecca heard Mrs. Andress behind her trying to reel in the over-stimulated kids.

"Come on, Dylan, let's get back inside … yes, Emily, it was funny … Amanda, do you have to go the bathroom?"

They walked to the truck, and Rebecca's dad handed her Doppler and Minden without a word.

As they drove to the next scheduled school, Rebecca chewed her lip and stared out the window.

"Think we'll work on a different script for the next visit," her dad said quietly.

A hot clump of distress sat in Rebecca's gut. *Is Dad gonna let me give the carnival rides now? What about racing?* She pressed a finger over each eyelid. *Puppy training is harder than it sounds.*

Chapter Seven

For two weeks Rebecca worked hard. She ran dogs, picked up poop twice a day, fed and watered the team every morning and night. She even set up an obstacle course for training the pups. Robin came over to help.

"So, why do the puppies have to run through the deep snow here? They're going to get scared." Robin pushed her glasses up and surveyed the scene like a Police Officer, hands on her hips.

"It's good for them to get a little stressed when they're young. They're learning to figure stuff out on their own. And when they run in the team, they won't get scared with new things." Rebecca liked showing off her knowledge of sled dogs to her new friend.

"Where do you keep your whip?"

"What?"

"You know, your whip for the dogs."

"I don't. Whip. My dogs!" Rebecca's lip curled in distaste, and she narrowed her eyes at Robin. "Maybe mushers *used* to use whips to snap in the air or something to get the dogs to listen, but we don't anymore."

"Oh." Robin shrugged. "I thought that's how you get the dogs to go where you want."

Rebecca seethed at the thought of what Robin suggested. "I use my *voice* to get the dogs to go where I want. They listen to what I say, and how I say it. It's called dog training."

Apollo sat by his house and stared at the girls. His big metal dish hung from his mouth.

Robin laughed and pointed. "Looks like the dogs are trying to train you too."

Rebecca relaxed and clapped her hands to the pups. "Pup, pup, pup, pup, pup," she called in a high falsetto. She took off as all the pups came charging toward her. They chased her and Robin as they climbed over ramps and through tunnels.

Robin probably wishes she had sled dogs, too.

That evening, Rebecca's dad called her into his office. She pushed open the door and stepped around the piles of books and papers stacked on the floor.

Her dad leaned back in the chair, pushing aside his manuscript on the dark, mahogany desk in front of him. "So, you think you're ready to give the rides?"

Rebecca swallowed and nodded. Then she met his eyes and grinned, feeling her dimple crinkle.

Her dad stood and laid both hands on her narrow shoulders. "It's okay if you changed your mind. It's a lot of responsibility."

Rebecca recognized his tone. *He's decided.* "Woo!" She threw her arms around his waist. "Thanks, Dad! I'm gonna go call Jackie."

Rebecca sat at the table the morning of the Winter Carnival, and tried to eat her Cheerios. Her stomach blurped and twitched. She couldn't decide if she felt thrilled or sick. Finally, she pitched the soggy cereal down the toilet.

Heather stood in the kitchen stuffing a cooler with sandwiches, drinks, and cookies. She pushed at the curly blonde hair spreading wild across her face. A wooden clasp held the rest of her curls at the nape of her neck.

Dad and I used to have fun with the dogs before she came along. We sure don't need her help now. Rebecca glowered at Heather's back. She thought again of her ship-bottle and fought the urge to hold it. When she looked into it, it helped her remember how her family used to be.

Rebecca's dad collected the new harnesses he'd ordered, and tied them in a bundle with a neck line. They still had not found the missing ones. A string of dog booties hung across the ceiling in the wood room like a colorful streamer. Each bootie attached to the next by its Velcro tab. The red, green and grey fleece — small, medium and large — looked festive.

"Bec, grab the booties, if they're dry," her dad said. "We might need to bootie them, if this snow turns icy. It'll be hard on their feet."

When they arrived at the carnival, Rebecca hardly noticed the throngs of people around them as they drove the dog truck through the parking lot to the trailhead. The Big Thunder Mountain ski hill rose up from the chaos in the background. Her mind spun previews of how her rides would go. She'd read that athletes perfected their routine by visualizing their whole event beforehand.

Tall ice blocks, chiseled into animals in various poses, dominated one corner of the parking lot. Snow sculpture contestants stood out against their red snow castles and bright green mermaids. Beefy horses stomped and snorted next to a wagon at the far end and children shrieked as they slid down a snow-slide.

Jackie and her mom waited for them at the trail. Jackie launched herself at Rebecca.

"Guess who's here!" She grabbed Rebecca's arm. "Chris saw the dog truck and he's coming over right now." She let go and waved her hands around like she was drying her nails. "How does my hair look?"

"I don't know, you've got your hat on."

"Crap." Jackie's hands flew to her head.

"Becca, get the drop line out," her dad said.

Rebecca opened the tailgate and pulled out two long chains. She snapped one end of a chain to an extension arm on the back bumper of the truck, then snapped the other end to the front bumper. It had six short chains attached along its length.

"Why is that called a drop line?" Jackie asked.

"It's called dropping the dogs when we let them out of their boxes. I don't know why. I'd never let the dogs drop."

Rebecca crawled in to the back of the truck again, and Jackie pounded on her calf whispering, "Here he comes."

"Hey, Rebecca," Chris said. Several other boys stood behind him.

Rebecca twisted her head around. She lay on her belly, reaching up for the harnesses. Stray bits of straw clung to her clothes and hair. Her butt stuck up in the air like a flashing neon sign. She closed her eyes. *Of all the bad timing.*

"Oh. Hey, Chris." *Smooth*, thought Rebecca. She caught a glimpse of his crooked smile, and felt her face get warm.

"Need some help?" he asked, leaning forward.

"No, I've got it." Rebecca slid out with the harnesses in her hand and hung them on the back of the dog box. She straightened her fur hat and noticed he wore his cool toque with the wolf on it. Brown curls stuck out the back.

"Where's the dogs?"

"They're all in their beds still, silly," Jackie cooed. "Come see. Here's Soho and Denali and Apollo and ..."

Jackie led them around the truck, reading off the names. Rebecca stifled a snicker. *Now she's interested in the dogs.*

Heather helped Rebecca's dad take the sleds off the roof, while Rebecca set up the sign she had made. She had used the stencil to paint, DOG SLED RIDES — $10.00. Rebecca glanced at the line of people already forming and sucked in her bottom lip. She clutched at her stomach, quickly realized that looked a little obvious, and brushed off imaginary lint from her anorak.

"Uh, we're still settin' up," Rebecca said to a lady trying to shove money at her.

"Well, I'm first when you are finally ready." The lady's pinched nose flared when a snowflake landed on its tip. She had on a long buttoned coat, black leather gloves, and a white beret perched, just so, on her coiffed hair. Black mascara smeared a little under her eyes with the damp snow building in the air.

Chris's crew seemed bored and wandered off.

Chris kicked at a lump of snow and glanced over his shoulder in Rebecca's direction. He hesitated a moment, then turned to follow the group. A relieved breath puffed out of Rebecca. *Don't need an audience right now.*

Rebecca opened the door of Apollo's box and caught him in the air as he leaped out. She bent and clipped him to the drop line.

"Seems you're a little busy Ribby," Jackie said, heaving a dramatic sigh.

"Have you seen my glove? I'm missing a glove." Rebecca searched the snow around the truck.

"Well, I'm going over to the snow sculptures. Diane said they're making Edward Cullen. I've gotta see that!"

"Take some pictures!" Rebecca called after her. Then she spotted Apollo poking his nose into a suspicious pile of snow and bent to retrieve her buried glove.

"How can you steal things when you've only been out less than a minute?" she asked him, smiling. "I don't need any practical jokes today." She stroked his cheek. "Just behave, and everything will be perfect."

Chapter Eight

"The trail is groomed in a circle for you," Mrs. Gower explained to Rebecca's dad. Rebecca moved close to listen. "You just follow around to the left. It goes through some trees for a short while and comes back here."

"Sounds good," her dad said. He stuck his thumb up at Rebecca. "Did you get that, Bec?" He turned back to Mrs. Gower. "Rebecca is taking the rides out today."

"Yeah, sounds good," Rebecca said in a voice that wavered just a bit at the end. Even with the chill air, she felt damp with sweat.

She continued dropping the dogs. Soho shook as soon as she came out, then peed. Apollo stretched his toes to scratch the yellow spot in the snow and craned his neck to sniff. Blaze started a howl, and to Rebecca's dismay, all the dogs joined in the chorus.

"Ssh!" Rebecca said, her gaze darting around at all the heads turned in her direction.

"Here's your first ride, Rebecca." Heather motioned at Mascara Lady, then silently clapped her hands behind the lady's back, grinning like a cheerleader. Rebecca managed to stop herself from rolling her eyes, and for her dad's sake, gave Heather a tight smile.

Once Rebecca and her dad had harnessed the dogs, Rebecca stood on the sled runners, and focused on not hyperventilating. She watched her dad hook up five more dogs.

I wonder what a heart attack feels like.

The crescendo of dog screams and wails grew with each new dog added. The sled bucked and rumbled. Mascara Lady daintily stepped into the sled with the aid of Rebecca's dad. Her thin lips pressed together.

"Will this seat be comfortable?" She asked as Rebecca's dad tucked a blanket around her tight enough to wedge her in.

"You bet." He nodded at her with a smile.

Rebecca pretended not to see Apollo leave a steaming pile of doo right on the trail. *Is that his idea of behave?* She hoped Mascara didn't see that.

The snub line that anchored the sled to the truck wasn't long enough. Rebecca had set the sled in front of the snow bank, and the dogs barked and lunged on the back side of the bank toward the trail.

It all comes down to this. Time to take control. Phase two of the plan is about to rip.

Rebecca's dad arched his eyebrows at her. She nodded and he let go of the leaders. Rebecca yanked the snub. The dogs lurched forward, slamming the sled up the snow bank. It launched off the top, and soared through the air like a parasailer behind a motorboat.

Rebecca clutched to the handlebar and watched the ground come toward them in slow motion. Finally, the sled landed.

Sideways.

The dogs continued their charge down the trail, dragging the tipped-over sled. Rebecca clamped the runner with one hand as she clawed at the snow hook with the other. She shoved it into the snow as she skidded along on her belly. Ice and snow sprayed her face. She heard muffled screaming coming from the sled. A white hat flew by.

Frantically, Rebecca leaned her whole body on the hook, driving it into the trail. It sliced through the thin snow cover. *Come on! Stop, stop, stop.*

At last, the hook caught. The sled shuddered to a dead stop.

Her dad, who had been sprinting behind, arrived panting beside her as she picked herself up. The dogs barked and lunged in frustration. Her dad pushed the sled up-right. His eyes widened when he saw Mascara Lady packed neck-deep in snow. And then his nose crinkled.

"Are you okay … oh, there's some … in your hair …" He trailed off.

Rebecca's cheeks burned as she took in the scene. The side-ways sled had plowed the same snow where Apollo had been.

"Ooooh … aaugh," Mascara Lady wailed. Black smudges ringed her eyes making her look like a surprised weasel.

"I'm so sorry about that," Rebecca's dad said. He helped her stand up so she could brush off. "We could give you a refund, or just continue from here, if you'd like. We've got the bugs worked out now." His eyebrows turned up in concern.

"Would you look at this … just look at this," she huffed. "I've never … I think that's enough dogsledding for one day."

Rebecca dropped her eyes as Mascara marched past. Her dad bent down and retrieved the hat, brushed it off and jogged to catch up.

Rebecca's whole face burned hot. *Well, so much for that.* She tried swallowing the lump in her throat. Her stupid hands wouldn't stop shaking. She stared ahead at the dogs with her shoulders slumped forward.

All that training and planning, down the drain. I'll never be allowed to run a race now. Maybe never be allowed to drive a team again. For the rest of my life. Yup. This is the end of my mushing career. Good thing Susan Butcher isn't here to see this. I bet she never dumped anyone into a pile of dog-doo.

When her dad came back, Rebecca studied the handlebar and blinked hard. She didn't trust herself to speak.

"Aw Becs, don't worry about it. That was my fault. I should've taken the time to attach the sled right." He had an odd little smile on his face. "But man, you sure held on, eh? Bien fait!"

Rebecca looked up in amazement. "You ... you're not mad?"

"Becca, you didn't let go of the sled. I'm so proud of you." He continued smiling at her with that odd expression. Like he was seeing her for the first time. "Are you ready for the next customer? The dogs are."

Rebecca stared at him, then her face broke into a slow grin. *Pro musher.*

Part Two
Yearlings

Chapter Nine

Twelve screaming dogs writhed on the long gang line. Their eyes crazed with desire to run. Their teeth flashed. Rebecca held Minden straight until the team leaped forward then reached a hand out to her dad on his way by. He grabbed her arm, helping her swing up behind him on the seat. The quad bumped and rolled in neutral as the dogs dug their claws into the frozen ground. For fall training, they used the quad, a four-wheeled All Terrain Vehicle with hand brakes.

They quickly gained momentum and zipped past a clump of birch trees, their bare limbs waving as they thundered by. The backs of the dogs rolled like waves on top of a wild sea. As always, the instant silence when they charged ahead rang in Rebecca's ears.

Rebecca imagined the dogs' delighted expressions were because of the glorious stretch of their legs, their long muscles working, the cool air in their lungs, the delicious smells of autumn leaf-rot and a million other secret smells only they knew.

Rebecca's gaze shifted between all four yearlings, pride glowing on her face. *I trained them.*

They started by running loose behind the sleds last spring. The pups weaved through the teams, quickly figuring out that the sled and dogs would run them over if they didn't stay out of the way. In doing this, they had watched the adults pull. Later, Rebecca ran behind them with a leash as they pulled a tire down the dirt road.

A rabbit darted across the road, and Minden let out a frenzied bawl of excitement. The yearlings clamored for a chase, their insane pulling sparking a fire in the adult dogs.

"Good dog, Apollo! Atta girl, Blaze." Rebecca grinned at the leaders as they kept the team straight, resisting the pull from behind them to chase the rabbit. She shook her head with a chuckle at the young dogs' savage galloping.

She thought training husky pups to pull must be like teaching a bird to fly. When Doppler felt the pull on his harness for the first time, she could see him thinking, *Wow, if I pull, I get to run. Fast.*

The first time she had hooked them up to the team was a different story. As she fought Doppler with the harness, both his front feet jammed into the same opening. He twisted around and lay on his back, then he shot up in the air and popped Rebecca's chin with his head.

"Ack! Would you settle down? Frig."

He spun around and around in wild joy, knotting the harness. Rebecca had to take it off and start over. She held him down to clip him in while he tried to kiss her. Once hooked, Doppler immediately jumped on Tarzan, caught his front foot inside Tarzan's harness and fell on the other side of him. Rebecca soon learned, the longer they stood still, the more tangled the mess.

But the exasperating first hook ups were behind them now, and Rebecca's heart felt full of sparkles as she watched them all run.

They pounded down the dirt road, bits of mud flying back toward the quad. Rebecca breathed in the crisp, forest smells as they silently bounced. She zipped her fleece up to her chin. Gray morning light filtered through the openings in the bright yellow tamaracks. The quad tires churned up mats of frost-coated duff on the ground.

Doppler pulled with enthusiasm, his head down and ears forward. Minden looked around as she ran, waving her tail in the air.

"Minden! Ahead, pay attention. That's it. Good girl." Rebecca noticed she didn't have to remind Doppler the way she did with Minden.

The adult dogs switched to their mile-eating

trot after their initial frantic energy released. They could sustain this pace for hours without tiring. The four yearlings had not learned this pacing trick yet, and continued their charge.

After almost an hour of running, a surge of power shot the quad forward as all the dogs suddenly broke into a gallop. Blaze and Apollo disappeared around the curve ahead. With such a long gang line, Rebecca lost sight of them until the quad rolled farther around the bend.

They must be excited being close to home. But then she saw what had sparked the dogs. A porcupine. Right on the road.

"Aah! Bouge, bouge, bouge!"

"Move! Out of the way!"

The prickly creature glanced over his shoulder at their shouts. Then he jumped in surprise when he spotted the massive dogs hurtling toward him.

The wheels locked up when Rebecca's dad squeezed the brakes. The dogs continued to scramble forward at a crawl, skidding the quad behind them. Rebecca felt a sickening déjà vu as she watched with her mouth open in a silent scream.

The porky ambled full tilt, in slow porcupine style, off the road. It was like watching a sprint race in a pool of thick oatmeal.

"Grab them!" her dad yelled. Rebecca snapped out of her frozen panic.

With a sharp cry, she jumped off the quad, and

dashed for the leaders. They inched toward Porky. Rebecca reached them in mid lunge and jerked them away by their neck line. Tarzan, in point position just behind the leaders, barked madly at it.

Porky stopped and brandished his spiky tail. His tiny black eyes glared at the dogs. Rebecca dragged the leaders farther away. Porky seized his chance and waddled off the road.

"On by, Apollo." Rebecca let the dogs go, but stood ready to grab them again if they decided to chase Porky.

Apollo gave one last, wistful look behind him then faced ahead. Rebecca's dad rolled up beside her, and she swung on again.

"That was close." Rebecca's breath wheezed in and out through flared nostrils. She wiped at the sweat and dirt on her forehead.

The dogs continued along the road until they rounded the last corner and rumbled into the yard.

"Good dogs." Rebecca praised as she patted her way down the line. The team stood with wide-mouthed grins. White froth coated their muzzles, and their tails waved as they gulped air.

While Rebecca rubbed down the dogs, her dad grabbed the bloody, chicken-laced water and bowls. They'd water the dogs on the line. Everything they did in training now was geared for The Thunder Dog, the one hundred fifty kilometer local race her dad ran every year.

Wonder if Dad's made up his mind yet. She had asked him about racing during a summer camping trip, but he just said, "We'll see."

He's probably watching to see if I can do it.

"Ouch." Rebecca looked at the back of her hand where Tarzan had pushed his nose. Something sharp had poked her. "Zany, look at me." She pulled his face out of his bowl and saw five quills sticking straight out of his nose. "Dad! The porcupine got Zany."

"Sacre bleu," he said, as he inspected the embedded quills.

Tarzan smiled at them and went back to his chicken broth.

"Well, I guess it could've been worse." Her dad chuckled. "We'll let them drink first. You want to get the pliers?"

As Rebecca searched the shed, the adrenaline of their close call gave way to anxiety. *What if I meet a porcupine by myself? If I knew what to do in an emergency, this would be easy. Dad's probably mad I keep forgetting things, too. I don't know where I put that stupid snow hook or the black leash. Or the harnesses. And the puppy pen door ... how's Dad going to trust me, or the dogs, if I can't remember important stuff? Heather's probably telling him not to let me race — I'm too young and irresponsible. I can just hear it.*

Once the dogs were back in the yard, Rebecca and her dad approached Tarzan. He smiled wide, peeling his lips back. A toothy pincushion, wagging his tail.

"Okay, try to do this fast, in the first shot. He doesn't know what we're going to do yet, so we've got the advantage," Rebecca's dad said.

He stroked Tarzan's head and held the dog's nose up toward her. She nodded, then reached forward with the pliers.

"Make sure you squeeze hard once you've got them, so they don't slip out."

Rebecca gripped the ends of the quills. Tarzan jerked his head back and Rebecca blinked at the five quills sticking out of the tool. She noticed Tarzan's nose had five little drops of blood forming at the end. He snorted and shook his head, pawed his nose, then smiled at her.

"Good job."

Rebecca flashed a relieved smile.

Her dad clapped her on the shoulder. "You might want to give the rest of the dogs a once over, just in case."

Rebecca saved Doppler for last, and when she was satisfied he was quill-free, she sat on his new house in the yard. When they outgrew the pen, each of the yearlings got his own house like the rest of the dogs. Doppler put his front paws on her lap and looked into her face.

"It's a good thing porcupines can't actually shoot out their quills, or everybody would've got it." She scratched Doppler on his chest absently. "We're not gonna get very famous if we don't race, Doppler. You think I should ask Dad again? Maybe he forgot."

Do it, Doppler gazed directly into her eyes. *You're great. I'm great. Let's go be great.*

Rebecca sighed, lay back on the dog house with her feet dangling, and studied the cloud shapes moving by. Doppler draped his chest over her belly, the heat from him sinking through her coat.

"You'll see, Doppler. When we finally get to race, it'll be epic."

Chapter Ten

The next morning, Rebecca woke before the alarm. *Something's different.* She squinted at the red digital numbers on her nightstand: 6:50 AM. She jumped out of bed and crossed the dark room, her bare feet cringing on the icy floor. Rebecca pulled the thick curtains away from the window and gasped.

Snow.

White blankets draped over the dog truck, piled on her old swing-set, and covered the whole driveway. Smooth white mounds perched by the truck where the lilac bushes usually stood. The brightness of it shone through her window, casting a muted light around her room. Rebecca rammed on the jeans and hoodie that were still in a pile on the floor. She grabbed the elastic on her nightstand and pulled her hair into a pony tail as she flew downstairs.

"It snowed," she said, as she burst into her dad's office. He sat at the computer in his blue plaid housecoat.

"Yup. Just listening to the radio to make sure your bus is still running."

"You said, when it snows, we can go camping with the dogs. Just you and me."

"I did. I'll take the snowmobile out to the camp site today to check it out." He leaned back with his coffee. "You want to call about your bus? It looks pretty deep out there."

Each winter they set up a walled prospector tent at a site about forty-five kilometers down the trail. They used it as a base camp for longer runs or just for fun camping trips. She loved the feeling of being on an adventure, sleeping away from home with the dogs, and the smell of the canvas and wood smoke.

Rebecca called Jackie. Her mom seemed to always know things involving school.

"Hey. So, are we having a snow day?"

"Apparently — nooo. But there's a crap-load of snow out there."

Rebecca had to cover the phone with her hand to muffle her laugh when she heard Jackie's mom yelling at her in the background.

"Aaaw, that's not fair," Jackie yelled back. Then she said into the phone, "Okay, totally not cool —

I hate that stupid cat."

"Chantal's cat?" Rebecca knew Jackie had little use for her younger sister's pet.

"Mom's got this new thing, every time she catches me saying c-r-a-p, I have to clean the disgusting litter box. It's not even my cat."

Rebecca giggled. *Whoa, she must be cleaning that thing a lot.*

"Okay, I'm gonna go gag myself with the armpit of a toad," Jackie said. Then brightly, "See ya on the bus."

When Rebecca hopped up the steps of the bus, she spotted Robin and staggered down the aisle toward her. She flopped into the seat in front of her friend and grinned.

Robin leaned over and pushed up her glasses. "Guess you'll start dogsledding now?"

"Yeah! Now that we've got snow, we can bring the sleds out and put away the quad."

"Did you watch Animal Planet last night? It was sooo good." Robin launched into a detailed description of the show. Her words faded into the background as Rebecca nodded.

Maybe I can drive the team to camp, just me and the dogs. Yeah. I'll bring all the dogs inside and let them sleep with me in my sleeping bag. Then I'll polish my dogsledding trophy that I won for being the youngest, bravest, most famous dog musher. Then we'll all eat chocolate coconut cookies in bed and not worry about the crumbs.

"Whoever made the crap-tacular decision to keep the buses running, should be fired." Jackie plopped down next to Rebecca. She shivered and flipped her hair. "Like, it's dangerous out there! *Look* at it." The tiny red heart painted on her nail flashed as she poked her index finger toward the window. "Icy much?"

"Yeah, I'm with you on that." Rebecca turned in the seat to face forward. "If it was a snow day, I'd be heading to camp with my —"

"Didn't you wear that yesterday?"

Rebecca looked down at the dark blue hoodie with THUNDER BAY in big white letters across it. "So? It's still lemony fresh."

"I'm just sayin'. I think Chris would notice if you wore something nice for a change — hey, Wheatgrass, this is a *private* conversation." Jackie glared at Robin behind them.

"Jackie! She's my friend …"

"It's a free country. I can sit wherever I like." Robin smirked and sat back in her seat.

Jackie turned back to Rebecca and rolled her eyes. She cupped a hand to hide her mouth and whispered, "She creeps me out." Then she straightened and reached to smooth Rebecca's eyebrow. "As I was saying … I could fix you up with a little eye shadow —"

"Not." Rebecca swatted at her hand and felt a twinge of annoyance over Jackie's jealousy. *I can have other friends.*

"Did you notice Chris's peach-fuzz? Like, he's going to have to *shave* soon."

"So how was the litter box?" Rebecca laughed as Jackie punched her in the arm. "Ow! And I wanna know, what does a toad's armpit smell like?"

The day crawled for Rebecca. She watched the white clock on the wall and tried to force the hour hand forward with the power of her mind. Strangely, that never worked.

By the time Rebecca hopped off the bus at the end of the day, she had another plan all mapped out in her head. A plan to clone herself so she could go to school and still be with the dogs all day. The first step would be to find some evil scientist who needed someone to conduct his cloning experiments on. She still had a grin on her face thinking of it when she went to find her dad.

"Hey, Becca, how was school?" Her dad shut the door to his office behind him.

"Yeah, fine, how were the trails? Can we go?"

"Trails are great. And the track from the snowmobile will make a nice base." He sauntered to the mud room and Rebecca followed after him.

"I set up the tent and stove." He poured water over the dog food. "And put up the bed platforms. Looks like we'll need more firewood, though."

"So, can we go?"

"Go? Where?" His mouth turned up a little at the corners as he stirred.

"Dad. Hello? Camping. You and me, you said."

"Ah. Camping. Well … I don't see … why not." Her dad's eyes twinkled. "How's this Friday after school sound?"

"Woohoo!" Rebecca jumped up and hugged her dad, then raced to the dog yard to tell Doppler.

"You may as well scoop poop while you're down there," her dad called after her.

Chapter Eleven

Friday afternoon, as soon as Rebecca's boots hit the ground off the bus, she sprinted toward the house. On the way up the stairs, she noted the sleds, packed and ready at the trailhead. When she burst through the door, her dad greeted her with a slip of paper.

Blaze	Tarzan	Apollo	Elsie
Soho	Doppler	Nitro	Ulu
Denali	Minden	Jade	Orbit

Rebecca studied the dog pairs and positions. "Which one is mine?"

"The one with Doppler, of course," her dad

said. "Look okay?"

"Yup."

"Do you have any homework?"

"Nope." Rebecca's mind flashed to the math book she had stuffed in her locker. *Famous mushers don't need math.*

"Okay, so go change, we'll have dinner after we get there. Unless you're hungry now?"

Rebecca ignored him and raced up the stairs, two at a time, to her room. She heard the dogs howling outside.

When Rebecca bustled out to the yard, she noticed her dad wore a headlamp strapped over his fur hat. *Oh yeah, it'll be dark soon, and camp's about three hours away.* Rebecca wheeled around and ran back to get her headlamp.

After the usual screaming, nerve-jarring, panicky hook-up, Rebecca once again stood on the runners of the chase team.

She waited a few moments to give her dad a head start, and then pulled the snub. They launched like a silent missile — heat seeking straight to the team ahead. They skied around corners, spraying snow behind them. They flew past black spruce and balsam fir, green needles stark against the snow. A sharp pungent smell hung in the air. The sled skipped over dips in the trail. Rebecca bent her knees with each bump.

When the trail veered west, she shielded her

eyes against the glare of the setting sun. The warmth of it on her face felt good against the cold wind. Ice crystals danced across the snow, making everything look alive.

Rebecca grinned wide as she imagined how wild she must look behind her team. *Here comes the greatest mad-musher the world has ever known. It's the Queen of Narnia running her wolves through the snow. No wait, that Queen was evil. It's Mowgli running with the wolf pack.*

Rebecca's fingers, wrapped around the handlebar, began to ache in the cold. She glanced down and remembered she only wore the thin gloves that were best for hooking up the dogs. She grabbed her big mitts that hung by their strings, twisted together behind her back.

Gradually, all six dogs broke from their lope to a brisk trot. "Good dogs, Minden, Doppler. You guys are good dogs."

They came to the field in time to see the team ahead disappear into the trees on the far side. The wind blew snow-snakes along the top crust. Blaze and Tarzan punched through large drifts that came up to their bellies. Rebecca's toboggan sled rode over top, and she jumped off the runners to run beside the sled. Running a hard-packed trail was so much faster than floundering in deep snow.

Hard, biting snow pellets stung her cheeks. She hopped back on the runners and pulled her neck dickey over her nose. Her lungs ached from breathing in the freezing air.

Only the strong survive out here, folks. Super-pro musher Bourdon and her amazing team are running in temperatures that freeze spit before it hits the ground. But she's not even scared. The fans are going wild.

When they reached the trees again, it seemed much darker. Rebecca peered through the approaching gloom. The dogs trotted effortlessly, eating up the miles.

Soon, full darkness settled over them. Rebecca saw a beam of light ahead, flash twice. She reached for the switch on her headlight and flashed two answering beams. The dogs were illuminated briefly, and she saw, with deep satisfaction, the tight tug lines. The wall of darkness closed in around them with the light off. In the dark, the sled seemed to slide faster between the trees. Rebecca belted out the song she planned to sing at her Idol audition.

If I sing loud enough, it'll scare away any monsters hiding in the dark shadows. Of course, there's no monsters. But the dogs don't know that. I'll keep them safe.

She noticed the dogs appreciated her amazing singing talent with the flick of their ears.

They followed the trail out of the bush and ran in the open along the tree line. The snow and wind had settled down, and the landscape appeared strangely lit. In the peaceful quiet of their running, Rebecca thought she heard a weird noise.

"Whoa, dogs." She stopped the sled and stood on the brake, listening.

The dogs dove into the snow, scratching their backs with little grunts of pleasure. She heard it again, above her. Rebecca looked up and sucked in her breath. "Wow!"

A wide band of green and pink light shifted and wafted across the sky like smoke. She watched the shapes form, bend and twist. She swatted her earflaps back and listened to the whistling, popping, and strange droning hum. *Is that the northern lights?* Whenever she had seen them before, it was usually through the kitchen window. She had never thought to listen.

The dogs were on their feet, looking at the sky. Doppler cocked his head a little, comically. Then they seemed to shrug and began barking for more running, less looking.

"Ready? All right!" Rebecca yanked the hook with ease and admired the awesomeness of her dogs and their joy in whatever they were doing.

Poor Jackie doesn't know what she's missing. Satisfaction crept into her smile. *Yeah. When I cross the finish line, breaking all known records, my fans will write songs about me.* Her thoughts, once again, shifted away from the moment to her future fame. She sang her way to camp, hardly noticing the trail lit up by dancing lights in the sky.

Chapter Twelve

"**D**id you see the lights?" Rebecca's dad asked, as soon as she pulled up.

"Yeah, so did the dogs." Rebecca stomped on the snow hook and bent to hug Doppler. "You should've seen Doppler, Dad. He pulled the whole time and only looked back once. He even tried to look ahead, past Blaze, like he wanted to be first. Then a squirrel ran across the trail and Zany wanted to chase it, but Blaze kept him running straight. Oh, I think we saw a deer running away through the trees. And man, the dogs were so awesome running in the dark; how can they even see? And we went through these huge drifts —"

"Okay, okay." Her dad laughed. "Let's get some chores done first. I'll drill a hole in the river for water and start feeding them. Could you unload the sleds and get dinner going?" He pulled the ice-auger out of his sled bag. "I brought moose-meat chilli, you just have to dump it in a pot and warm it up on the camp stove."

They worked together, and soon the dogs were curled up on beds of straw, tied in a line to the stakeout cable. Rebecca had stoked the wood stove so full it felt like a sauna inside the tent. Mitts and hats hung, steaming as they dried. The fire snapped and popped while they drank creamy mugs of hot chocolate.

Twelve harnesses, tied by a neck line, hung from a nail in the spruce frame. The smell of wet dog drifted around the tent.

"Better get some sleep, we'll run the big loop tomorrow." Her dad pulled out his winter-weight sleeping bag and laid it on his wooden platform.

Rebecca dug her finger into her mug and scooped out the last of the chocolate on the bottom. "Same teams?"

"Yup, those dogs seem to run well for you."

Rebecca smiled with pleasure and crawled into her sleeping bag. It crinkled as she moved. She left the zipper open so she wouldn't sweat in the warm bag. As soon as she closed her eyes, she felt the pull of sleep.

She jolted awake. Midnight. *What's that noise?* This time, it wasn't the northern lights. She sat up and listened.

"Woooo." The distant howling of wolves.

Rebecca reached for her headlamp. She shined it on her dad, and he clenched his eyes closed.

"Hey."

"I hear something," Rebecca whispered. "I think its wolves." She knew they sometimes attacked dogs.

Her dad lifted his head and listened. "They're far, far away. Go back to sleep."

Rebecca tried to fall back to sleep, but soon she heard them again. This time they were closer. Their haunting, eerie voices filled the darkness. Little hairs on the back of her neck bristled straight out. She rolled over and ducked her head inside her bag. *Doppler and all the other dogs are outside, tied to that cable.*

Again, she grabbed her light. "Dad. The wolves are closer."

"Rebecca, they're miles away —"

The wolves howled again. This time, it sounded like they were right outside the tent, completely surrounding them.

"Dad!" Rebecca's heart thumped hard. Her light, a meek line through the inky blackness around them. The beautiful, sorrowful voices of the wolves rose and fell together. She heard nervous rustling coming from the stakeout line.

"Hmm. I'd better check on the dogs." Her dad

got up and pulled on his boots. His bony knee-caps nearly poked through his red long johns. He grabbed his anorak and pushed aside the door flap.

The cheery crackling and warmth of the fire was gone. Rebecca sat in the dark alone. She heard the crunch of her dad's footsteps as he walked around the tent.

The howling stopped abruptly.

Her dad's light glowed through the walls of the canvas as he pointed it toward the trees around them. The low whimpers of the dogs shifting in their beds made Rebecca get up, too. In her worry for the dogs, she forgot to be afraid.

"I don't see anything," her dad called through the tent walls. "They did sound close though, eh?" He muttered in French under his breath.

Rebecca shivered in her long johns as she rooted around for her pants. She dressed, grabbed her headlamp, and went outside. The cold night air stabbed tiny forks at her cheeks.

"Rebecca, go back inside. The dogs are okay."

"The wolves … the wolves won't come if we're out here, right?"

"No, they won't come, don't worry."

"Okay then, I'm gonna sleep out here. Out here with the dogs."

"What? Don't be silly, it's too cold. Let's go back in." Her dad put his arm around her and tried leading her back to the tent.

"No, Dad. I'm sleeping beside the dogs." *Those wolves are just waiting for us to go back in. I'm not letting any more animals attack my dogs.*

Her dad heaved a sigh that acknowledged the stubborn tone in her voice. She wouldn't let this go. "Okay, we'll get some ground sheets. At least it's not snowing."

He pulled two tarps from their sled bags, and gave one to Rebecca. She arranged hers next to Doppler, half on his straw, the other on top of the snow. The dog watched with interest, but did not uncurl his body. His bushy, white tail covered his black nose. Only his eyes moved as he watched her slide into her winter sleeping bag and zip up to her chin. She tightened the bag's hood over her head to lock in her body heat.

"This is fun, eh, Doppler? It's like a pajama party." When Rebecca spoke, her frozen words hung in the air around her head.

"You warm enough over there, Becca?"

"Yup. Snug as a bug in a rug. Wait till Jackie hears about this. She's not going to believe me."

"You are a strange, stubborn girl, Bec." Her dad adjusted his hood over his head, pulled the toggles tight until only his nose peeked out and lay down. "Bonne nuit, mon petit chou."

"Bonne nuit, Dad."

The next morning, as the first pink rays crept up the back of the low hills on the far side of the clearing, Rebecca tried to sit up. Her bag stuck to the snow. She rolled to break the frozen grip of the suspiciously yellow ice clinging to the side of her bag. Rebecca narrowed her eyes at Doppler.

"Hey! You peed on me."

Doppler rose and stretched each part of his body separately. Front legs reaching forward, back arched, claws digging in, then back legs straight with each toe splayed out. His eyes closed in a delicious, gaping, tongue-curling yawn, complete with sound effects. And then he shook.

With that done, he jumped on Rebecca, licking her face. *Hi! Are we going running now?*

"Augh." Rebecca's dad groaned and sat up. White frost from his condensed breath hung around the rim of his bag like a beard, making him look like a disheveled Santa. "What a night."

As each dog stood and stretched, Rebecca and her dad climbed out of their bags. They watered the dogs, broke camp and packed the sleds in record time. They sat on their sled bags eating grilled cheese sandwiches made with french toast. She glanced at her dad and caught him watching her with that peculiar smile. *Is he still monitoring me? Did he notice all the chores I just did?*

On the trail, Rebecca sang loudly to her dogs.

A smug smile lit her face. She watched the low

alders lining the trail flash past. She listened to the tinkling of the dogs' neck lines, breathed in the cold, invigorating air, and felt quite proud of herself. She was running her own team of six dogs that she had hooked up, slept with outside, and saved from wolves. Her careful plan had worked.

Dad's gonna tell me I can run a small race on my own. Heather won't be able to stop it. I wonder if Mom will come watch.

She began working on her wave, preparing for the crowds of fans. *Should I do a Queen wave — too snobbish. Maybe a full arm wave — too childish.*

She was turned half way around on the runners, waving, when they suddenly hit a stump. The sled tipped precariously on one runner. Rebecca scrabbled frantically for a grip. The sled teetered. It balanced for an eternity, like a basketball circling the rim. Rebecca watched her worst fears play out in slow motion.

Tip.

Grab.

Slip, and then the sled toppled over.

She fell hard.

"NO! Blaze, Doppler, come BACK!" Rebecca leaped up and dashed after the team. The sled, unfortunately, had righted itself, and happily slid along behind the dogs. She pumped her legs faster, panic zipping through her veins. She begged the dogs to stop. The team charged ahead, climbed a small hill, and disappeared over the crest.

Gone.

Rebecca stopped and dropped to her knees. Hot tears coursed down her face. Her lungs burned. Her hands shook. She pulled in ragged, deep breaths.

Get up! Get your team. They need you. She wiped her nose with the back of her glove and hauled herself up. As she jogged down the trail, a woodpecker hammered a tree beside her. He went about his day, uncaring of her complete disaster.

"Stupid, stupid, stupid," she chanted.

Chapter Thirteen

Rebecca ran. She reached the top of the hill and saw nothing but more, empty trail. She kept running, stopping only to peel off her hat and neck dickey. She rounded another corner, still no sign of the team. She tried to stop her mind from showing horrible scenes of the dogs balled up, fighting, blood everywhere, Doppler screaming. Over and over it played for her.

How could I be so careless? The dogs were counting on me to keep the gang line tight. Blaze is probably wondering where I went. The dogs are all doing their jobs, and I'm out here running in the snow like an idiot. Worse than an idiot — idiots don't know any better.

Compared to running with the sled, her progress was frustratingly slow. Her feet slipped a little with each step, like running in soft sand. It took forever to reach a stump, an eternity to pass a tree. If she got the team back, she'd never take for granted how fast they flew down a trail. How effortless it felt to slide past rocks, outcrops, and willow clumps.

She crested another hill and her breath huffed out in a frosted cloud. Her team stretched out on the trail, happily rolling and biting snow. The snow hook, buried into the trail, looked as though a forest elf had come, set it, and then disappeared.

Rebecca, red-faced and panting, grabbed the sled and stomped on the hook. *It must've bounced off the sled and landed in the trail. So lucky.*

Steam rose from the top of her hatless head. She trudged to Blaze and collapsed on the snow beside her. She buried her face in Blaze's neck fur.

"I'm sorry," she choked out. Only then, when she knew the dogs were safe, did she start to shake. Tears spilled down her cheeks as she gulped loud, ragged breaths. Six pairs of eyes watched her. Blaze poked her cold nose in Rebecca's ear and snuffled loudly.

"Ah, that tickles," Rebecca said, giggling. She wiped her nose and stood. The team rose to their feet as well. When Rebecca walked back to the sled, the dogs began to leap and scream.

Ten minutes down the trail, they rounded a corner, and Rebecca saw the other team stretched out. Her dad bent over Ulu, inspecting her feet. He looked up as Rebecca's team approached.

"Are you okay? What happened?" He took in Rebecca's tear-streaked face. "Are you hurt?"

"No." Rebecca couldn't even look at her dad.

He started to walk toward her but hesitated. He scanned her dogs, her sled, then gave a quick nod. He turned back to his sled, and bent to pull his hook. "Ready? All right."

They continued down the trail. Rebecca's dogs, oblivious to the near catastrophe, ran well and happy. No one saw the black cloud that hovered just over Rebecca's bouncing head.

At home, as soon as the dogs were looked after, Rebecca ran to her room. She shut the door, savagely grabbed her headphones and jabbed at the play button. She snatched her ship-bottle and lay on her bed staring into it, imagining the three of them that day. Laughing. Eating ice cream.

Her eyes burned and she tore her gaze away to look up at her wall. She wished she could tear down Ms. Butcher and her perfect huskies. *If I could just move. Ugh. Everything aches, my head hurts, my feet are throbbing, my legs are stiff.*

She lay thinking on her bed for a long time, too numb even to cry. By the time the knock on her door came, she had her plans made. She'd move to Tahiti. She'd drink Tahiti Treat all day and work on her tan. It didn't snow in Tahiti. It almost made her feel better.

"Hey, is there room at the pity-party?"

Rebecca stuffed the ship-bottle under her rumpled quilt. "Sure."

Her dad sat on her bed and removed her headphones. "So, I want to talk to you about something. Are you ready to listen?"

Here it comes. I'm not gonna be allowed to touch a dog again. Well, I don't care.

"Bec, every musher loses their team at some point in their career."

What? How the —?

"Is that what happened?"

Rebecca stared at the wall and nodded.

Her dad sighed and patted her knee. "Well, sometimes accidents happen. I lost them a few years ago, don't you remember? When I broke my collar bone?" He absently rubbed under his shirt collar. "But I bet you learned something today, didn't you?"

Rebecca scratched her nose.

"That's all we can do, just keep moving forward and hopefully learning as we go. You know what Papa Bourdon used to say to me when I was young?" He raised his eyebrows, waiting. When she didn't respond he continued. "He'd say, 'You'll never feel good about yourself if you don't do anything hard.'"

Rebecca pointed her toes, then rotated her ankles trying to get rid of the muscle cramps. She glanced at him.

"You're a musher, Bec. And mushing is hard. But, you're one of the most dedicated, caring mushers I know, and the dogs run well for you because of it." He paused, waiting until she looked at him again. "That's why Heather and I agree that you're ready to run a race. We were going to wait for your birthday to surprise you, but … I signed you up for the Thunder Dog."

Rebecca sat up straight. "Huh?"

"What? You weren't going to give up on your dreams that easy, were you?"

Her mind whirled trying to make sense of what he was saying. "The Thunder Dog? I'm running the Thunder Dog?" *And Heather agreed?*

Her dad nodded, and grinned. "The race is in six weeks, so you'd better get that hang-dog look off your face and buck up."

Rebecca jumped up and leaped on her dad. "Woohoo!" She tried to moonwalk across the floor, tripped on a pair of socks and almost fell backward. She resorted to springing up and down, her sore muscles suddenly completely healed. "I'm running the Thunder Dog!" As she bounced, a slow dread snuck up her back and hooked into her brain. *I'm running the Thunder Dog?*

Chapter Fourteen

Now that Rebecca would be racing, she needed to pick her string. She invited Jackie over to help decide which dogs would be on the team.

"I want to bring all of them," Rebecca said. She sat cross-legged on her bed with a pad of paper and the words MAIN TEAM across the top. "But I can only take six."

"Well, who's your favorite?" Jackie shrugged like it was an easy decision. She flipped through Rebecca's CD's.

"I can't bring just my favorites, I have to think of which dogs will race good. Like, I'll have to bring Apollo and Blaze to lead." She wrote their names on the pad. "They've done the race before, so hopefully we won't get lost." Rebecca's stomach flipped at the thought.

"I don't even know why you want to do this. I

wouldn't need this kind of stress in my life." Jackie pulled out a CD and inspected the back.

"Not helping, Jackie."

"Okay, okay. So you need four more. What about Doppler, you keep saying how amazing he is." Jackie caught her reflection in the CD cover and pursed her lips as she flicked at a tiny red mark on her chin.

"We're s'posed to wait 'til the yearlings are older before they race. All the noise and stuff might freak them out. They might lose their happy attitude. Attitude is important." Rebecca looked pointedly at her friend. Jackie rolled her eyes.

Rebecca tapped the pencil on her teeth. "I'll need strong dogs too, maybe Denali and Tarzan." She wrote their names down.

"You've got a lot of nasty looking dogs there. Isn't Tarzan the one with the teeth? And Apollo is one mean dude, speaking of dogs with attitude."

Rebecca smiled.

"What if the newspaper wants your picture or somethin'? No one is gonna want to go near you. How 'bout that pretty white dog — Soho."

Soho is pretty with her white-fox face and black nose and eyes. She might lead too, if I need her.

"Yeah, that's a good suggestion." Rebecca raised her eyebrows at Jackie.

"What? You didn't think I'd know about this stuff? I could be like, your rep."

"I'll take Elsie too, they like to run together."

"Just direct all your PR stuff to me, I'll take care of it." Jackie flicked her hair. "Crap, Ribby, we're gonna be so famous. Oh! I almost forgot." Jackie grabbed her purse, a chunky white bag with the word PRINCESS across it in sparkled letters. She searched through her assorted stash and finally pulled out a small bag. "I got you a gift for the race." She passed it to Rebecca who gave her a delighted smile.

"You can put it on your sled, and think of me while you try not to die horribly out there."

Rebecca opened the paper bag and pulled out a blue, oval sticker. It read:

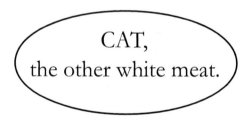

Rebecca burst out laughing and fell back on her pillow. "Ugh, that's so disgusting, I don't even know what to say."

"You're welcome." Jackie's devil grin made her laugh harder.

That evening, Rebecca searched her backpack looking for her homework, and found a wrapped package. She pulled it out and read the sticky-note:

This is ur real gift. I'm so glad ur my bff. Even tho I think it's weird, it's also cool u have a dogsled dream and don't let anything stop u. Good luck at ur race.

J.

Rebecca tore off the wrapping, and stared at the framed picture. She recognized it right away from the day at the carnival. Jackie had come by while she gave rides and snapped a picture of her waiting for her next customer. She stood on the runners, beaming a wide smile. Her face was flushed and seemed to glow. White frost hung on the fur of her hat next to her temples. The dogs gazed into the camera with wide grins and frost around their muzzles.

Rebecca's eyes widened, and she glanced up at the poster of Susan. Her photo looked almost the same, except Rebecca wasn't wearing a racing bib. A warm tightness seeped through her chest. She shoved aside her frogs on the shelf, and placed the frame in the center. *Yeah.* She stepped back and tilted her head. *It is cool.*

For the next month, Rebecca ran her team, and

her dad ran the B string. They practiced passing, and running at night, but mostly they just enjoyed the time on the trails. After every run, they fed and watered the dogs on the line, just like they would during the race. They mixed long runs one day, then short fun runs the next. As each week passed, Rebecca crossed it off on her desk calendar with a red marker. She almost forgot about her past mistakes. Her dogs ran well, and they were fast. Her dreams of fame became clearer in her mind.

The Thunder Dog would start on a Saturday and run through Sunday. On Wednesday night, Rebecca brushed her teeth hardly believing there were only three more sleeps before race day.

In the morning, Rebecca rolled out of bed, shucked on her clothes and padded downstairs. As usual, she went straight to the window to see what the dogs were doing. Nothing stirred.

They must all still be sleeping in their houses.

She climbed into her insulated coveralls, pulled on her dog yard boots, and stepped outside. The dogs didn't move. No one poked their nose out at the sound of the door slamming. No morning howls. A cold, panicky fear shot through Rebecca as she ran toward the yard. The closer she got to the yard, the stronger her panic.

Then she stopped dead. Her face became p

as snow. Her mouth hung open. All her limbs weakened, and she dropped to her knees, staring.

The dogs were gone.

Every last one of them. Disappeared.

For a long moment, Rebecca's gaze bounced from one empty house to another. Her mouth closed, sagged open, then closed again. The white parts of her eyes flashed. Then, the shock and disbelief made their way to her brain and she jumped to her feet.

"Dad! Daaaad." She flew back toward the house, a hot stabbing fear in her guts. She burst through the door. "DAAAAD!"

"What the … Bec, what's wrong?" Her dad glanced out the window, saw the empty dog yard, and jerked back to her face. "What happened?"

"D-dogs … dogs are gone …? Rebecca pointed out the window.

"Heather!" Her dad sprung toward the mud room and began ripping into the gear. "I'm taking the snowmobile to look for the dogs."

Heather appeared, wide-eyed in her pajamas and bear-paw slippers.

"Can you go in the truck and start knocking on doors? I'm heading up the trail." He grabbed his helmet and stormed out the door.

"Rebecca, you want to stay here by the phone? I'll call on my cell if I find anything." Heather dashed toward her bedroom.

"O-Okay." Rebecca felt numb and her tongue didn't seem to work properly. *How can they be gone? I fed them and put them to bed. They were all there. Did I leave all of them un-clipped? Augh! I can't remember.* Terror squeezed her heart.

Rebecca heard the snowmobile roar out of the yard. She heard the truck chug out of the driveway. And then she heard nothing at all. No dog barks, no howls, no chatter as they sometimes did when they argued with their neighbors

Rebecca stood in the middle of the room in her winter gear, the deafening sound of silence surrounding her. She covered her face with her hands and sobbed.

Chapter Fifteen

"**P**ull it together," Rebecca said. She swiped the back of her hand across her nose. "Think."

She peered out the window again at the empty yard. *What could have happened?* Her eyes narrowed. *There's no way I screwed up all their clips.*

Rebecca marched out the door to the yard.

She scanned the ground for paw prints. *All these dog tracks could have been from any of the times we ran them this week. It hasn't snowed in a long time.* Rebecca bent and picked up Apollo's chain. She inspected the clip, snapped it a few times, then looked down at the ground again.

Then she saw them. Boot tracks in the snow leading to the trees.

She dropped the chain and followed the tracks. Her heart began to trip when she saw the direction they were heading. Straight to Robin's house.

Rebecca tromped toward her neighbor's, stormed up the back stairs, and pounded on the door. Her hands curled into fists. Her blood raged through her brain. *What does Robin have to do with my dogs?* She stood at the door a moment, then saw a figure out at the road. Robin waiting for the bus. *Is it still that early in the morning? So much has happened.*

Rebecca sprinted toward Robin, her face hot, her temples pounding.

"My dogs are gone! Do you know anything about that?"

Robin sneered at her, her lips curled up like yesterday's scab. The intensity of her stare gave Rebecca a shiver of fear.

"I set them free. Dogs should not be chained up and forced to pull a sled all their life. What kind of life is that? I thought they'd come home with me, like the dog did last year, but they left."

"You! It was you who let Blaze go?" Rebecca's thoughts whirled. "What about the harnesses? The puppy pen?"

"Yeah, I took your harnesses. I took a lot of gear. I thought if you didn't have them, you couldn't make the dogs run. But that didn't work. I tried to let the puppies go too. I guess they weren't smart enough then to leave. But, as you can see now, they've all had enough of being your slaves." Robin gave her a satisfied smirk. Icy tendrils of hate wrapped around Rebecca's shock.

"Agh! Of all the stupid …" Rebecca's fingers gripped her own hair. "You don't know anything. Where did they go? Do you have them?"

"They all ran down your trail. I don't know where they went."

"And now, they could all get hurt, or run out onto the road and get hit by a car, or get lost …" Rebecca couldn't finish with the ball blocking her throat. She couldn't stand to think of the million dangers for her dogs. Something else niggled in the back of her brain. Something wasn't right about Robin's story.

The bus came into view and rolled to a stop in front of them.

"You getting on here today, Hon?"

"N-no, I'm … I'm not coming," Rebecca managed to say.

Robin hopped on the stairs and turned for one last smirk at Rebecca. "The dogs are happier when they're free. Trust me. You'll see."

Rebecca stood on the side of the road and watched the bus drive away. Her thoughts swirled. Relief to finally know it had not been her misplacing everything and forgetting to shut the pen door. Terror for the dogs' safety. Seething fury at Robin and her warped sense of reality.

"Augh!" Rebecca screamed at the sky. She didn't know what to do next or how to deal with the mix of emotions. She wanted to kick something. A satisfying image played out in her mind of running to school and finding Robin. *I'll pick her up and drop her in — say, a big pit of venomous snakes. "Don't you want to free the snakes?" I'll ask. Yeah. But first I'll dip her in festering mouse turds, then …*

Rebecca's hands balled into fists as she suddenly realized what had been bothering her.

Why hadn't the dogs barked? Huskies don't bark much, not like guard dogs. But they'd bark if someone they didn't know came into the yard. Someone they didn't know. Rebecca's shoulders slumped. She had introduced them to Robin. *Maybe that's why Robin always wanted to help with the dogs.*

Rebecca choked out a sob, and shook her head. She hugged her elbows tight to her body. *Where are they?* she wondered.

She remembered she'd told Heather she'd wait by the phone. She turned and sprinted along the road to her house. She stood on the top of the stairs and looked out over the dog yard. The quiet, emptiness of it was strange. Spooky. As empty as her heart. Rebecca cupped her hands around her mouth and whistled as loud as she could. She listened for a moment and heard nothing.

"Doppler, Dooopleeerrr," she hollered into the wind. Nothing.

She went inside and stared at the phone on the wall next to the kitchen. *If someone calls, I'll need something to write on.* She grabbed a pen and notepad and put them next to the phone.

It didn't ring.

Her head pounded, and she felt sick to her stomach. She paced in front of the couch, fists clenched, still wearing her boots and coveralls.

Please, please don't run onto the highway. Rebecca tormented herself recalling her past conversations with Robin. *Were there any clues? Anything I should have picked up on?* She felt even more sick and collapsed on the couch. She curled up in a ball.

My first ever race, ruined now. Everything's ruined. She thought of the first time Doppler ran in harness. Of how it felt to stand on the back of the sled, racing through the woods. Of the way she felt after a run, visiting with the dogs, and their happy faces. The wonderful doggy smell of them. Their joy at life. *Ruined.*

A shrill ringing jolted Rebecca up. She dove for the phone.

"Rebecca, nothing yet. Have they come back?"

Heather's voice irritated Rebecca. She shouted into the phone. "No! They're not back yet, and you shouldn't come back either. My dad and I were happy here. He doesn't need you. You just ruined everything. This is all your fault!" She slammed the phone down. Then slammed it again. Sobs choked her throat. She raced upstairs to her room.

When she burst through the door, the first thing she saw was her ship-bottle. She picked it up and, with all her strength, flung it to the floor. It exploded with a loud tinkling smash. Her momentary satisfaction almost immediately gave way to remorse.

She stared at the little ship, broken and laying in the shattered mess, just like her dreams. The words, CANADA'S WONDERLAND, seemed to leer at her with red teeth.

Rebecca turned and fled back downstairs, through the house, and out the door. She didn't stop running until she was part way down the trail to the beaver pond. She sat on a log and let herself cry. Huge, racking sobs poured out of her. The noise of it seemed to hush the forest around her. No birds called, no trees rustled. After a long while, she wiped her eyes and looked around.

Why didn't Mom like dogs? Why did she have to move so far away? She wished her dogs were asleep right now in the yard. Wished they were all still preparing for the race.

Rebecca felt the cold from the melting snow on the log seeping into her skin, and stood to wander down the trail. She heard the truck chugging into the driveway at the house, but no dog songs erupted to welcome it. She imagined Heather's face when they spoke on the phone.

Why did I say those things? It isn't really Heather's fault the dogs are gone. It's not so bad having her around. She makes Dad laugh. And I don't really think Mom wants to come back. At the last thought, Rebecca's bottom lip trembled, but it was a small relief to admit something she'd been hiding from herself. She imagined the disappointment in her dad's eyes when he found out what she'd said to Heather, and felt her cheeks burn.

She found a wide pine leaning, waist-high, off the trail. She layered spruce boughs on the flat crook of it and climbed onto the nest.

I can't go to school today. Not ever.

Rebecca curled up and fell asleep with the image of Doppler's smiling face in her mind.

Much later, a snowmobile roaring past on the trail, woke her, and she fell backward off the tree. *Maybe he found the dogs!*

She shivered and wondered how long she'd been sleeping as she crawled stiffly to the trail. She raced home to meet her dad. When she got to the yard, she could see him through the window, but could tell by the way his shoulders slumped that he hadn't found them.

"Rebecca! Where have you been? Heather and I've been worried sick."

Guilt shoved at Rebecca's heart. "I … I was trying to find the dogs."

Her dad eyed her. "Go get dressed for school. It's not too late for me to take you in. And it will help you take your mind off things."

"Dad, it was Robin. From next door. She came and let all the dogs go."

"What? Why would she do that?"

"Because I let her." Rebecca turned away from the confusion on her dad's face. With a hollowness in her chest, she trudged up the stairs. *This day can't get any worse, may as well go to school.*

Chapter Sixteen

Rebecca avoided Jackie and Robin for the rest of the afternoon at school. She put her head down and pretended to do homework on the bus when Jackie tried talking to her.

"What's up, Ribby?"

She didn't want to tell Jackie about the dogs. Saying it out loud would make it feel more real. "Nothin', just trying to read." Rebecca ignored the hurt look in Jackie's eyes.

When she got home, Rebecca tore down the driveway. The dog yard sat barren like an abandoned park. Empty houses. Ghostly silent and still.

"I'm heading out on the snowmobile again to look for them," Rebecca's dad said when she came in. "Maybe they went to camp."

Rebecca nodded and dropped her school pack on the kitchen table. When she couldn't hear the snowmobile anymore, she crept into her room with a broom and dust pan. Little shards of glass lay around the tiny broken ship.

She dumped the whole thing into the trash just as Heather came home from work.

"Hello? Anyone here?" She paused when she saw Rebecca and sighed. "Hey."

"Hey."

"Your dad still looking for the them?"

"Yup."

"I'll go drive around again." Heather sat down at the table across from Rebecca and rubbed her hands over her face. "You know Rebecca, I'm upset about the dogs too. But it won't help to take it out on the people around you."

"I know."

"Those things you said really hurt my feelings."

"I know." Rebecca struggled with the baseball in her throat. "I just … I'm scared for the dogs."

Heather slumped in her chair. "So am I. I love the dogs too. I love this whole family, you know." Her voice dropped to a soft hush. "You and your dad are my whole world, Rebecca. I'd do anything for you. You know that right?"

A sob escaped, and then Rebecca couldn't hold back the flood. Heather stood and pulled Rebecca into her arms. Rebecca clung to her.

"I'm scared all the time, not just 'cause they're missing. I'm scared I can't run the race. I'm scared even when I'm running the dogs." Once she started talking, it felt as if she'd just flung open a door. She breathed in a fresh breath in relief of finally telling someone. "What if I'm like my mom? She's sort of afraid of dogs. She never wanted to go near them. I want to be like my dad." Rebecca cried harder. They stood together beside the table until she drew in a ragged breath. She pulled away and swiped at her nose.

Heather looked her in the eye. "Rebecca, when people do things even though it scares them, that's called courage. You *should* be a little afraid of racing. It means you know what you're doing." Heather brushed a loose hair from Rebecca's face. "I don't know your mom, but I don't think you're like her. I don't think you're like your dad, either. You are just like yourself. You make up your own mind who you are." She peered at Rebecca with a little smile.

Rebecca smiled back and felt lighter somehow. "I didn't mean those things I said. I'm sorry."

Heather nodded.

"Okay. Well, don't forget your cell phone, I'll wait here. We'll find them, right?"

"I hope so, Bec."

Rebecca heated a can of soup for supper, though she didn't feel like eating. Doing homework was useless, she couldn't imagine being able to care about school again. She didn't want to sing, or dance or listen to music. She just wanted her dogs back safe.

She ate automatically, her mind and body feeling numb. She rinsed her bowl and glanced outside. The moon shone a mournful light across the snow. Rebecca flicked on the dog yard lights and slipped outside to stand on the top of the stairs.

"Dooooppler!" She cupped her hands around her mouth and called again as loud as she could. "Pup, pup, pup, pup," she chirped.

The empty dog yard mocked her. Not a thing moved. No howls or barks in the distance. She turned and shuffled back inside.

Should probably call Jackie and tell her. Jackie had made plans to be at the start and end of the race. Rebecca had overheard Jackie telling Samantha about the surprise poster she planned on holding up with Rebecca's name. She sighed and wrapped her arms around her stomach.

Just as Rebecca reached for the phone, she heard a thud. She jerked her head toward the door and listened. Thud, thud. Coming from the door … the door!

Rebecca raced to the mud room. She swung open the door. Doppler, who had been throwing himself at the house, burst through the doorway and into her legs. Then eleven more dogs mowed him over as they charged into the house.

Rebecca's eyes widened like it was Christmas

morning. Her whole face lit up as she threw back her head and screamed and laughed. Twelve dogs rushed around the room, whining, panting, growling, leaping. Empty feed buckets crashed to the floor, while coats were pulled off hooks and trampled. Rebecca heard nails tapping furiously on the hardwood floors, the couch springs squeaking from bodies jumping, wet slurping coming from the bathroom, house plants toppling over, kitchen cupboards slamming, something that sounded like cereal spilling, she didn't even care one bit. Her dogs came back. She had called them, and they came home.

The next evening, as Rebecca and her dad prepared to leave for the mushers' meeting, they made a disappointing discovery.

"She's not going to be in any shape to race tomorrow," her dad said, squeezing Blaze's front leg, and bending it gently. The lead dog had come home from her ordeal with a limp. She whined softly and pulled her leg away from the probing exam. Rebecca's dad rocked back on his heels and rubbed at his neck.

I'm gonna kill her. I told her this would happen. "I'm gonna call Robin …

"That's not going to help, Bec. What's done, is done. I've already spoken with her mother. She will deal with it." He stood and draped an arm over Rebecca's shoulders. "Right now, you have to decide who to take from the B string."

Rebecca ran through the dogs in her mind. *Soho will have to do in lead. At least Apollo will be there to guide her. But who to run with Elsie?* A tangy thrill ran up her back. *He can do it, I'm sure of it. He's not afraid of anything. Nothing bad's gonna happen to him. I hope.*

"I'm gonna take Doppler," Rebecca said with a decisive tone.

Her dad raised his eyebrows, then nodded. "You're the musher."

"And I'm gonna ask Heather to handle for me."

"Wow. Um. Okay." Her dad flashed a smile, then recovered and nodded nonchalantly. "Good for you, Bec. I think she'll like that."

She grinned and felt the last of the heavy load she'd carried for so long, crumple away. She stood straight. "Come on Dad, I don't wanna be late for the meeting."

Chapter Seventeen

"**W**e're gonna be fine, Denali. See, I'm not nervous at all." Rebecca straightened after trying to coax Denali from under the truck.

I hope he can't tell I feel like I'm about to hurl. She knew the dogs sensed her emotions and took their cues from her.

I don't blame him for hiding, it's where I want to be right now. She eyed the chaos surrounding them. A wide assortment of dog trucks lined the parking lot. Hundreds of crazed dogs barked, squabbled, whined and leaped on their drop lines. Some veteran dogs relaxed in the afternoon sun, and some hid under their trucks. Mushers and onlookers darted through the dirty slush. Smells of urine-soaked straw, anxious dogs, and jittery mushers hung in the air.

A voice boomed out from the loudspeakers on

top of the announcers truck. "And wearing number thirty-eight, our very own Ken Healy is back. He'll try to top last years amazing time of …"

"Ribby! There you are." Jackie weaved her way toward Rebecca, flicking her hair over her bright red coat. "Crap, do you know how long I've been looking for you? What a circus!" She gave Rebecca a quick hug.

"Yeah, pretty crazy, eh?"

"What number are you?"

"Twenty-seven. So, it'll be a while before it's our turn." Rebecca wished she had picked a smaller number from the hat at the musher meeting. She'd have to watch twenty-six teams leave before her, all three minutes apart. She felt pretty sure she was growing an ulcer.

"Why can't you do a normal race, like a five or ten k?" Jackie asked. "Then I wouldn't have to wait so long for you to come back."

"That's a sprint race — it's totally different. These are mid-distance dogs." Rebecca turned back to Denali and knelt down, tilting her head to look at him.

"Okay. Well … when's your turn you think?"

"I dunno, at least an hour."

"So … you mind if I go with Diane to check out the crappy games booth?"

Rebecca hardly looked up, waving her hand as if she shooed a fly.

"I'll be back — I know where you are now," Jackie turned, jumped out of the reach of Tarzan's muddy, outstretched paw, and hurried away.

Doppler pawed at Rebecca and she slid over to him. His hot tongue slobbered her chin.

"Oh, nice." Rebecca laughed and pushed him away a little to scratch his ears. "We're both running our first race together, Doppler. I'm so glad you're here."

"And this year, our youngest competitor wears bib number twenty-seven. Rebecca Bourdon, the local girl from …"

"Hey, Becca, hear that?" her dad yelled from a couple of dog trucks away. He strode toward her with bouncy purpose. Several people standing near Rebecca turned to stare at her. She felt her face get hot. A fluttery, spinning pest seemed to have lodged in her stomach.

"Dad," Rebecca said when he got closer. "I've got to pee again." She ran to the line of Port-a-potties and tried to hold her breath as she squeezed inside the closest one.

When she returned to the truck, her dad was waiting with a camera crew.

"Here she is." He clapped Rebecca on the shoulder. "Becca, these reporters are here to do a piece on you."

Rebecca's lunch nearly made a repeat showing. "Um … Okay."

The lady with the microphone approached, motioning for the camera man to follow. "Hello, Rebecca. I'm Alana Grant with T-Bay TV. I was hoping you could answer a few questions for us." She flashed bright white, perfectly straight teeth behind her pink lipstick.

"Sure." Rebecca wished her face would stop heating up. *Oh, man, Jackie's gonna be disappointed she missed her chance at PR.* Rebecca shoved her hands in the front pocket of her anorak and studied her mukluk laces.

Alana smiled warmly. "It's okay to feel a little nervous at first."

"I'm not nervous."

"Good, we'll start then. Ready?" Alana cleared her throat and nodded to the camera man. "We're here at the start of the great Thunder Dog dog-sled race, and we're talking to one of its youngest competitors this year — Rebecca Bourdon." She turned to Rebecca, "How long have you been training for this event?"

"Um, like, since my whole life … ah, September I guess." Rebecca's panicked gaze rested on the dogs, and she caught Apollo staring at her. She thrust her shoulders back, raised her chin, and met Alana's eyes.

"What do you like best about dogsledding?"

"That's easy — the dogs. They're so smart and funny. They're like my friends. If I'm in a bad mood or something, I just sit with them for a while, and I feel better. It's way better than even a pet dog. We work together — like, I depend on them. And they know it. You want to meet 'em?" Rebecca bounded to Doppler.

Alana and the camera man followed. Doppler flung his front paws on either side of Rebecca's neck, his head nearly the same height as hers. He tried to lick her.

"This is Doppler." She put her arms around him. Her eyes gleamed. "I trained him. He's only a yearling — that's like a teenager."

"What do you need to train a sled dog?"

"Well, you need a sled … actually you can do it with skis … I guess you also need trust. We have to trust each other, like a team." When she said it, Rebecca realized it was true. The dogs ran well because they trusted her.

Rebecca introduced the other dogs. Tarzan did his best to entice a pat showing Alana his own fine, straight teeth.

Camera man tapped his watch at Alana.

"Well, Rebecca, I see you are an expert in the sport. Do you have any advice for other kids wanting to get involved?"

"It's hard work taking care of them, but really worth it." Rebecca looked directly at the camera. "The main thing is keeping the dogs safe. From everything. Even from people who don't understand how much the dogs love to run. If you make sure the dogs are happy, they'll show *you* how to be happy. Do that, and they'll pull you in to their happy dog world."

Alana paused for a moment, seemingly mesmerized by Rebecca. Then her camera face popped back and she cleared her throat. "Okay. Spoken by a young lady who knows what she's talking about. Thank you, Rebecca."

When they left, Rebecca's dad grabbed her up in a bear hug. He swung her in half a circle with her feet dangling and Rebecca laughing.

"Wow! You were amazing." He gave her a mock punch on her arm. "Once you started talking about the dogs."

Rebecca hummed to herself as she checked her gear. *I hope Robin watches the news tonight.*

Most of the crowd milled around the race chute once the teams started leaving. After twenty teams had gone, Rebecca stood at the back of the sled. Her dad, Heather, and three volunteers held her team. A race marshal motioned for them, and they skidded and dragged through the parking lot. Each volunteer pulled back on a section of gang line while the dogs humped forward. Rebecca jogged beside the sled to keep the runners from being scratched in the mud.

They lined up behind six other teams. Every dog barked hysterically. Behind her, Rebecca heard a dog fight break out and a musher yelling. She didn't look back.

The announcer blared more information but she couldn't listen. Every muscle in her body felt as if it were being zapped with electric volts. The energy of the dogs hung in the air. She felt it cling to her. Above the cacophony, she heard her heart pounding in her ears.

"Ribby!" Rebecca heard a familiar voice and scanned the crowd, until she saw Jackie waving wildly. She ran toward Rebecca with Chris. Jackie stopped, pointed at Chris's back, and mouthed something that Rebecca couldn't understand.

"Hey, I tried to find you before." Chris's soft voice brought Rebecca's gaze to his. He stood with his crooked smile, his chest puffed out as he took a deep breath. For a moment, they just looked at each other. And then he leaned in, so close she could smell his Juicy Fruit gum.

He shoved a little box at her. "Here." He shrugged, turned and bolted away.

The dogs moved ahead as another musher left. Rebecca's team entered the narrow path of snow fencing with sponsor banners on both sides. Three teams bounced ahead of her. She glanced behind her at the berserk, barking dogs, foaming like rabid science experiments from *Lilo and Stitch*.

The crowd stood behind the banners, cheering and calling out.

When they stopped, Rebecca leaned on the handlebar and opened the box. A small pin with a dog wearing a halo nestled on a piece of paper. The note read:

GOOD LUCK REBECCA.

Rebecca felt a warm flutter trickle down her spine and shoot through her stomach. She slipped the box with the note into her sled bag, and stuck the pin into the collar of her anorak. She smiled.

"Three, two, one, GO!" the crowd chanted. Air horns blared. People cheered as team twenty-five took off down the chute.

"Six more minutes," her dad yelled.

Rebecca shook out her arms, and rotated her head like she'd seen Olympic athletes do. She took deep breaths and tried to pretend she was somewhere else. Her hands shook. Her stomach twisted into knots. Her knees were jelly. *What was I thinking? I should have my head examined.*

Rebecca's team leaped in the air. They jumped over each other. Soho screamed. Tarzan dug a feverish hole. Stringy goobs flew. They scrabbled with all their strength against the men that held them. Slowly, they moved into the chute. Two burly guys grabbed the stanchions of Rebecca's sled.

"We gotcha," said Burly Guy on the right.

Rebecca stared down the open chute ahead of them. Breath held. She stood on a rumbling rocket launcher.

Now, now, now, barked Apollo.

Great, great, great, barked Doppler.

"Three, two, one, GO!" The sled lurched forward. Rebecca's grip tightened. The dogs bolted down the chute. Past her dad. Past the crowds. Toward the silent, unknown trail ahead.

Chapter Eighteen

Apollo and Soho barreled after team number nineteen. The thrill of the chase drove them on at a gallop. Rebecca let them go. She blinked rapidly to clear the tears freezing in her lashes. Their speed caused the wind to sting her face.

"Trail!" Rebecca called as Apollo shouldered past the musher. He glanced back then leaned to the left to steer his sled over. Rebecca watched her leaders run beside the other team with their eyes faced forward. Doppler reached his nose toward the new dogs to greet them as he passed.

"Doppler, on by!" Rebecca smiled as his head snapped forward. The other team continued running straight ahead, making it easy to pass them. Gradually, Rebecca and her team pulled away from them, and her heart squeezed with pride.

For several miles they continued to pass teams,

and a few passed them. Rebecca chuckled at the wide-eyed glance Doppler threw over his shoulder as another team approached. He seemed to dig in, wanting to go faster. Rebecca could tell the dogs knew they were racing by how long it took for them to switch from a lope to a trot.

The surge of speed after spotting a team ahead, the galloping chase, the pass and the gradual pulling away, leaving the team behind, became less and less frequent. They slipped past tall pines, granite outcrops, frozen marshes with tall cattails standing straight as if watching the race. The groomed trail snaked ahead, curving around a red pine stand, their long shadows stretching across the snow.

After a couple of hours, as she did in training runs, Rebecca stopped the team for a break. She tied the sled to a tree with the snub line.

"Let's see what I've got in here for you." She rummaged in the sled bag. The dogs watched her from over their shoulders. When she pulled out a bag of frozen, ground chicken chunks, Apollo demanded, *now, now, now.* Tarzan pranced.

Rebecca hurried to the front of the line and tossed a chunk, twice the size of a fist, to each dog. Apollo snatched it in mid air and dropped to the ground to gnaw at it, turning his back on Soho.

Rebecca doled out the rest of the treats then dug around in the sled bag for a Power Bar and thermos. She munched as she collected her thoughts.

A few Gray Jays called, breaking the stillness of the forest around her. The deep silence helped her settle. A patch of birch trees, their papery white trunks crowding together, hid her view of what was around the next bend. Pink wisps of cloud hung low in the darkening sky.

Rebecca wiped at her nose, which ran freely in the cold air. She was finally here. On the race trail, alone with the dogs. Her contented sigh was quickly followed by a tightening in her guts as her thoughts raced to what lay ahead. *Eighty kilometers is a long way to the checkpoint. It's farther than where we went camping last summer — and that had taken an hour riding in the truck.*

She knew exactly how long it took because she had gotten car sick, and they had to pull over on the way. Rebecca shuddered and held her stomach.

It should take us about six hours. Then another five hours after the checkpoint. At least I won't be car sick.

The last purple hues of dusk faded darker as Rebecca and her team charged down the trail again. Trail markers blazed yellow on the trees and Rebecca breathed a little easier thinking she could stop worrying about getting lost.

She dug into the sled bag for her headlamp, being careful to grip the handlebar with her other hand and watch for hazards ahead. Losing the team again was definitely on her to-don't list.

They ran through the night at an easy pace.

Paws skimming the trail, tongues out. Happy dogs. When Rebecca felt a familiar surge of power, she slapped on her light and scanned the team. They looked ahead, seeming to focus on something on the trail.

Oh, no! Not a porcupine! Frantically, she searched the trail, but saw nothing. *A beaver? Please, don't let it be a beaver.*

The dogs continued to gallop forward. And finally, Rebecca saw it.

A sandwich.

Her muscles relaxed a little, her mind straying out of control in relief. *What kind is it? Jam and pickles? Maybe salami or, ew … hope it's not spam. Please don't let the headlines read, YOUNGEST MUSHER FOILED BY MYSTERY MEAT.*

In the second that it took Rebecca to play guess-the-sandwich, Apollo lunged, grabbed for it, and missed. Tarzan dove at the same time as Denali did. The two dogs locked into a vicious, snarling ball.

Rebecca threw down the hook and bolted toward the fight. "NO! Stop it. Zany, enough!" She waded right into the flashing teeth and savage screams, and pulled Tarzan off Denali.

"Denali … give me that." Denali gulped the prize as Rebecca reached in to take it. The sandwich had disappeared. Blood, beginning to freeze, framed Denali's mouth like a clown's red grin.

"Apollo, ahead!" Rebecca yanked the leaders around to face down the trail and gave everyone her sternest look. *Someone ahead better be wondering where their supper went. I hope that wasn't some strange racing strategy.* She hopped back onto the runners with shaky legs, the adrenaline of the dog fight receding. *Hey, I just broke up a dog fight. By myself! I didn't even have to think about it, not like when Apollo got bit. I really am becoming a good musher.*

The revelation that she could trust herself to do something when needed, was so sweet, she burst out singing.

The rest of the run sliced by and before she had time to wonder how much farther, Rebecca saw lights ahead and the dogs' ears perked forward. She glanced at Doppler and a grin spread across her cold face. His straight tail and tight tug line warmed her insides. Rebecca thought he must be enjoying the different trails and new smells. Seeing his confidence, Rebecca felt a little more brave.

"Rebecca!" A voice called from the shadows. Heather took the leaders' neck line and led them toward their truck parked under a flood light. Her dad was there making broth.

"Well, how'd it go …?" His voice trailed off as he noticed Denali's face.

"Awesome!"

A volunteer with a clipboard hurried over, crunching on the snow, "You have to sign in."

Rebecca pulled off a mitt and signed her name, putting a smiley face at the end.

Rebecca ladled out bowls of the chicken broth. Steam rose from the tepid liquid into the cold night air. Most of the dogs drank eagerly. Elsie tipped her bowl to eat the gobs of chicken off the snow.

"Aw. You're supposed to drink it, dummy."

"Miss, you have your required gear?" A giant man wearing a bib with RACE MARSHAL across it stood near her sled.

"Yeah, it's all still in there," Rebecca said.

"The vet's coming over to check your dogs and you'll be allowed to leave five hours from now, okay?" His short, thick fingers opened the sled bag and sifted through the gear.

After the mandatory gear, vet and time checks, Rebecca brought her dogs to the straw beds Heather had prepared next to the stakeout line. By the time she fed them a warm supper of dog food mixed with meat and fat into an oatmeal-like consistency, she wobbled on her feet as she bent over the dogs' bowls.

Her dad led her to a large tent. A sign hung over the door, QUIET, MUSHERS SLEEPING. They moved the door flap aside and picked a cot out of a row, being careful not to wake those already sleeping. The tent had no heater, but with the mushers inside and the absence of wind, the warmth hit her like a downy quilt. She picked at the frozen laces of her mukluks, but then decided to just leave them on.

"You rest now. I'll wake you when it's time."

Rebecca crawled onto the cot and bunched up her anorak for a pillow. *What a day.* The TV interview seemed like years ago. The chaotic race start, the dog fight, the dark trail and worry over what lay ahead all swarmed through her mind.

Her eyes closed, snapped open when she heard the dog songs through the tent walls, then fluttered closed as her mind drifted along fluffy, white trails lined with sandwiches.

Chapter Nineteen

"**H**ey, it's one-thirty. Half an hour to leave."

Rebecca sat up and gawked around owlishly. *What ... oh yeah ... crazy dog race ... middle of the night ... head examined ... right.* She shrugged on her anorak and crept outside.

A blanket of muted sounds had settled over the little encampment. A few stragglers were still coming in and some teams were quietly leaving. Rebecca pulled down the earflaps on her hat to ward off the cold wind.

"How do you feel?" her dad asked.

Rebecca's head snapped up at the tone in his voice. "What's wrong?"

"They're calling for some nasty weather to-night." He hesitated and rubbed the back of his neck. "We can pack up now if you want. You've already run a great race. I'm so proud of you."

"No way! What happened to your 'if you never do anything hard' speech?"

"Okay. Okay. I'm just saying, you have a choice." He clapped her on the shoulder. A puff of frozen air rose in front of his face. "You get the dogs up and watered. I'll get the vet and a race marshal." He gave her a wry half-grin, but she didn't miss the cloud of worry in his eyes. He turned to find the vet for the mandatory check-up.

Rebecca didn't want to think about quitting. She also didn't want to think about being on the trail in a storm. She shook her head, decided she'd worry about it later, and crunched to the stakeout line. All six dogs stood, shook, and wagged their tails at her approach.

"Hey, guys. Are you ready to do that again?" She bent over Doppler, then dropped to the straw and wrestled with him. His brown eyes sparkled when he looked into hers.

This is great! We're on an adventure, Doppler seemed to say.

"You're having fun, eh? Not scared are you? What a good dog." Rebecca spent time praising each dog. Heather passed her a steaming bucket, and she watered the dogs as she checked them for any signs of stiffness. Heather loaded the sled with another sack of dog snacks.

Once the dogs and equipment had been checked by the Officials, they hooked up the team.

The dogs whined and pawed like they'd just had two weeks sleep.

"Half way there, Bec. How do you feel about that?" her dad asked.

"Great!" She used Doppler's word.

"Just be careful. And ... trust the dogs."

"See ya," Rebecca called as they ran off the edge of the friendly flood lights and into the dark night. She blinked her eyes to adjust, gripping the sled blindly for a few minutes. Gradually she noticed the brilliance of the stars and the light the moon cast on the trail. She saw the outlines of the dogs. Snow blew across the trail, obscuring it.

This isn't so bad.

Too soon, the wind began to gust. It sent sharp ice pellets into Rebecca's eyes. It picked up strength quickly. Rebecca strained to see the trail. She clicked on her headlamp and felt as though she was strapped inside a video game. Snow flakes, illuminated by her headlamp, whipped past.

Our hero, Rebecca Bourdon, has been sucked into a wormhole folks. She's speeding through to another dimension. What will she find at the other end? Perhaps a world ruled by forest elves? Rebecca flicked off her light.

She squinted into the dark as her eyes adjusted again. She strained to see the leaders. Something felt wrong.

Is Soho limping? Rebecca stopped the team. She bent over Soho, shining her headlight on her.

"Are you hurt, girl?" She felt along each leg, squeezing slightly and bending, watching Soho's reactions. Rebecca's snow-covered brows furrowed as she turned over the dog's left front foot. A delicate, raw rub-wound glistened pink between Soho's toes.

"Oh, no! Soho, why didn't you say something?"

Rebecca ran back to the sled and tore through her gear. She ripped off her gloves and with bare hands, found the jar of salve and the bootie bag. The savage wind bit at her exposed skin. She raced back to Soho, dropping to her knees beside the dog. She dug a finger into the cold goop and spread a thick layer over the wound. Then she slipped a bootie on each of Soho's feet and secured them with their Velcro straps.

While she tended to Soho's feet, the storm grew in strength. Ice pellets pelted her. She heard them bouncing off her anorak. The wind tore at her breath. It burned her throat, and sliced her lungs with tiny knives. Rebecca gasped and ducked her chin into her dickey. She tucked her hands under her armpits and turned toward the sled, hesitated, and then turned back to the dogs.

Better make sure. Rebecca knelt before each dog and examined every foot. She splayed out their toes to check between. Wearing only thin gloves for dexterity, she secured booties on every dog.

By the time she was through, her fingers ached

with cold. They barely responded as she jammed them back into her outer mitts. She hopped around trying to get her blood moving. When she pulled the hook, they continued down the trail.

The vicious wind grabbed at Rebecca's clothing. Her hood snapped sideways around her face. Howling gusts nearly shoved her off the sled. The dogs appeared and then vanished like wraiths in the hard snow swirling around them. Rebecca shone her light on Soho, shielding her eyes from the storm. The dainty dog ran, but with a limp.

What should I do? Panic and indecision pounded in Rebecca's head. *I can't let Soho run with a limp, that could cause a shoulder injury. But if I put her in the sled bag, I can't ask Apollo to lead by himself. In the dark … with this crazy storm.* Her teeth bit her lip. *Tarzan? No, they tolerate each other, but won't run together.*

Rebecca hunched on the runners trying to protect her face from the icy blasts. The gusts seemed to suck her breath away. She swallowed down the desperation that rose in her throat.

An idea came but she quickly dismissed it. *That's too much pressure for him. He's just a baby. He's never even been in lead during training. Lots of dogs get stressed running in front of the whole team.* She'd seen some dive off the trail or refuse to run. Not all dogs could lead.

Rebecca shone her light on Soho. The dog bravely trundled forward with an awkward gait.

She glanced back at Rebecca.

Rebecca stopped the team. She unhooked the dog and set her gently in the sled bag, clipping her neck line in so she wouldn't jump out.

"Don't worry, girl. You rest here. What a good dog." Rebecca stroked her white head. "You've done enough today."

Soho sat calmly in the swirling snow, like she knew her race was over.

Rebecca unhooked Doppler. "Well, you think you can do this?" The wind snatched her words away. She clipped his neck line to Apollo, who glanced at him with a perfunctory huff. Apollo's focus was on the trail ahead, the next bend, the exciting new smells. Even in a raging, blowing blizzard, he seemed to hate stopping.

Rebecca walked backward to the sled, watching for what Doppler would do. He stood up front, looking over his shoulder at her.

"Ready? All right!" Rebecca yelled, over the shrieking wind. All the dogs leaped forward in unison. Rebecca shone her light to Doppler. *He's running straight.* He glanced over his shoulder once then focused his attention on the trail ahead.

Dark wind whipped snow across the trail, across Rebecca's vision, making it impossible to tell if they were following it or lost somewhere in the blizzard. Freezing snow melted on her right cheek and burned. Somehow, the lead dogs stayed on the trail and continued trotting. It occurred to Rebecca that without the dogs, she would be completely lost in this blizzard and would probably die. Doppler appeared to know that she needed him. He almost glowed with importance.

Slowly, Rebecca relaxed. They were not lost. No one was freezing to death. The dogs seemed to be enjoying the cold. After a while, Rebecca even began singing to the dogs. She stood tall on the runners and noticed the tree trunks weren't quite so dark, the bare branches not quite so spooky. Their gnarled fingers that had reached out to rip her from the sled, now stretched out, pointing toward the pale light emerging through the aspen.

The snow had stopped some time ago. She stood with one foot on the runner and pedaled with the other, pushing the sled forward. As she pedaled, they broke from the narrow trail into an open field. Sunbeams crawled above the trees and burst out to touch her left cheek. The savage wind had blown out. Only a few flakes swirled around.

With the brilliant light of the sun, every tree branch sparkled with hoarfrost. Rebecca watched the rays reflect off millions of diamonds all over the snow. She forgot the stress of the last few days, the near disasters, the blinding storm. She sucked in her breath at the sight of her dogs running in a line surrounded by glitter. *This is so worth everything I've done to get here. I belong here.*

The dogs perked up suddenly and began to pull harder. Moments later, Rebecca heard it. The sound of traffic. They rounded the corner, all the dogs breaking into a lope. Rebecca saw the crowds. Her dad and Heather waved madly, Blaze on a leash sitting beside them. She saw Jackie cheering with Scott and Chris. *Wow. Jackie must be freaking out sitting so close to Scott.* Jackie waved her banner above her head. *And is that Robin? Yes.* Robin had a bag draped over her shoulder and was dejectedly picking up trash. Rebecca let out a giggle at the sight of Robin bending, holding out some nasty food wrapping, and stuffing it in the bag.

Soho sat up and peeked her head out of the sled bag. Doppler gaped around and began to prance with his tail up like he was royalty. Rebecca imagined Susan Butcher's spirit in the crowd, cheering.

Doppler looked over his shoulder at Rebecca and their eyes connected. Pride swelled in her chest so strong, she felt like the cartoon Grinch when his heart expanded — her joy too big for her to contain. Her throat constricted. Something tickled behind her eyes. The tense band of muscle between her shoulders finally released for the first time in over five hours.

Through the fog of air horns, cow bells, and her own blood pumping in her ears, she heard the announcer's voice, "And here's number twenty-seven, Rebecca Bourdon, as she finishes her first ever dog sled race. I wonder what's next for this young musher? Perhaps the Iditarod."

The Iditarod! Now there's a good idea. Her thoughts strayed as she imagined the parade they'd have in her honor when she arrived in Alaska. Maybe even a marching band. She quickly shook her head, forcing herself to do something she'd learned from the dogs. Live in the moment.

Just ahead, the finish line coaxed her forward. She jumped off the runners and ran beside the sled as it crossed. Rebecca Bourdon, Pro Musher, faced the crowd and raised her arm in a victory cheer. And then she turned to hug her dogs.

Glossary of terms:

Alaskan Husky - a mixed breed of dog with bloodlines originating in Alaska and bred for speed, toughness, and endurance.

Checkpoint - a designated place along a race where teams get checked by officials to make sure they are following the race rules.

Drop line - a portable chain or cable that the dogs are attached to when not on the gang line or in the dog truck.

Gang line - the line that attaches to the sled by a bridle and runs between the dogs. All the dogs are attached to the gang line.

Gee - a command to turn right.

Haw - a command to turn left.

Musher - a person who runs sled dogs.

Neck line - clips onto the dog's collar from the gang line to keep the dogs straight.

On by! - a command to go straight, past an obstacle.

Pedaling - when a musher stands on one runner of the dogsled and pushes the ground with the other foot in a forward motion. Used to help the dogs pull the sled.

Skijoring - wearing skis and being towed by a sled dog.

Sled bag - a fitted bag that is tied to the inside of a dogsled.

Snow hook - a heavy metal claw attached by a rope to the gang line. It's designed to dig into the snow when pulled on to keep the dogs temporarily in place.

Snub line - a line attached to the bridle that runs along the dogsled and can be tied to an unmovable object to anchor the team.

Trail! - a signal from a musher to the team ahead that they are about to pass, to ask them to move over on the trail.

Tug line - attaches to the back of a dog's harness and to the gang line. It's how the dog's power is transferred to the sled

Team positions

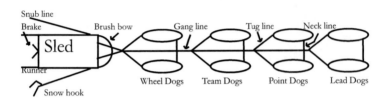

Snub line
Brake
Sled
Runner
Snow hook
Brush bow
Gang line
Tug line
Neck line
Wheel Dogs
Team Dogs
Point Dogs
Lead Dogs

Resources

Mush with PRIDE (Providing Responsible Information on a Dog's Environment) - www.mushwithpride.org

Mushing Magazine - www.mushing.com

Sled Dog Central - www.sleddogcentral.com

John Beargrease Sled Dog Marathon site - www.beargrease.com

Yukon Quest Junior Mushers site - www.yukonquest.com/site/jryqmushers

Zuma Paw Prints - Official canine reporter for the Iditarod - http://iditarodblogs.com/zuma/

~Author~

Terry Lynn Johnson

Terry's passion for the outdoors evolved while she paddled Quetico Provincial Park as a Canoe Ranger. One winter she worked for a dogsledding company, and eighteen huskies followed her home.

Dogsled Dreams is her debut novel about those quirky dogs that entered her life and heart.

Visit her at:
www.terrylynnjohnson.com

Acknowledgments

Many thanks to my beta readers Jackie White, Linda Provence, Diane Andress, and Doug and Sandy Johnson for reading the first draft. Thank you also to my critique partner Paul Greci for wise suggestions and an eagle eye. Thank you to Joyce White, who pushed me, and who I know will be just as excited as me when this book comes out. And to my amazing editor Keri Rouner who offered words of encouragement when needed and a good swift kick when I needed that too.